COUNTDOWN...

Hector plugged in the terminal and dialed the number that put him in direct contact with Tri-State Chemical's in-plant computer. All was in order. A moment later the words appeared on his terminal printout. SIGN ON, the computer said.

Hector typed in the identification key he had used so many times before when he worked at the plant, then fed into the terminal the chemicals he wanted mixed together and the sequence. When he had the last chemical added, the terminal was silent a few seconds, then typed back to him: WHAT PROCESS?

He turned off the machine, unplugged it, and put the phone back on the hook. He opened the blinds on the motel window and stared a quarter of a mile across the field at the chemical plant. He wasn't sure how high it would blow, but there would be an explosion of considerable force when that last chemical was added to the other mix. It was a chemical bomb. How big the whole thing blew depended on the quantity of certain other chemicals in the immediate mix area and in the storage tanks and bins. If there were sympathetic or chain-reaction explosions, it could be huge.

Hector checked his watch. There could be a ten- or twelve-minute batching procedure working when he countermanded the computer's mix run. He would have to wait. . . .

THE PENETRATOR SERIES:

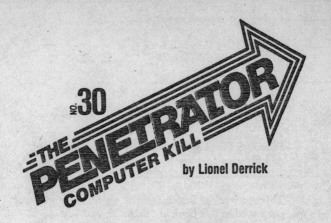

NO. 30

THE PENETRATOR

COMPUTER KILL

by Lionel Derrick

PINNACLE BOOKS • LOS ANGELES

Photo for Combat Catalog illustration courtesy of Ahl Foto.

PENETRATOR #30: COMPUTER KILL

An original Pinnacle Books edition, published for the first time anywhere.

First printing, March 1979

ISBN: 0-523-40270-8

Special acknowledgment to Chet Cunningham

Cover illustration by George Wilson

Printed in the United States of America

PINNACLE BOOKS, INC.
2029 Century Park East
Los Angeles, California 90067

TABLE OF CONTENTS

COMPUTER KILL

PROLOGUE

> "*Revenge is the nectar sweetening the lovelost, but the essence diminishes into chaotic fumaroles of disillusioned agony in the afterdeath.*"
> —John Fischer Burney

To some the Penetrator is an angel of mercy; to others he is the ultimate judge with a scale of justice in one hand and a blazing .45 automatic in the other.

The Penetrator did not plan to become a modern Robin Hood, striving to right the wrongs of a worldwide Nottingham Forest; he did not want to become a man feared and hated by criminals and mobsters, hunted by the police, a man who had to snatch what pleasures and happiness he could in brief moments of time.

It all evolved from this nation's participation in the Vietnam blunder, where Mark Hardin served as a soldier, and soon developed into an expert marksman with all of the army's weapons and devices of death, a specialist on trips inside enemy territory, and a man in constant demand to lead raids. He was described as that one in a million who is a natural fighting man, an instinctive combat genius who knew what to do and when to do it. Mark Hardin became an exceptionally expert manhunter.

He took special training and soon returned to 'Nam, where he uncovered a gigantic black market operation that involved many high ranking U.S. Army officers, including a general. Mark felt the army would cover up the affair, so he told his story to a wire service reporter who broke it on front pages around the world.

Mark was immediately relieved of his duties, and shortly after that a gang of thugs from the black market group caught Mark alone and beat him savagely, leaving him for dead. Only Mark's remarkable will to live and his determination brought him through. Eventually he was returned to the States, most of his injuries mended, and he was discharged from Letterman General Hospital in San Francisco.

Discouraged and weak physically, he talked to his old coach at UCLA, who promptly took Mark to a friend of his in the desert near Barstow, where the ex-USC geology expert, Professor Willard Haskins, had built a hideaway mansion inside an old borax mine. There Mark met David Red Eagle, and the ancient Indian nursed Mark back to vigorous health.

One day the old Indian announced that he was sure Mark was part Indian, and they began tracing records in Los Angeles County, where Mark had grown up as orphan and ward of the court. They soon discovered he was half Cheyenne. David Red Eagle, also a Cheyenne and a medicine chief, began teaching Mark the secrets of his background, the Indian ways of life and of fighting, and at last the fabled rituals and skills of *Sho-tu-ça,* the Indian medicine-magic of the Cheyenne Dog Soldier.

During this time Professor Haskins' niece, Donna, stayed at the large "Stronghold" facility. She helped Mark go into Los Angeles to search records to find his background. The two became good friends and fell in love. Within a few days Donna was dead. Their probing of records had come too close to some clandestine Mafia operation in Los Angeles and the godfather had ordered both young people silenced.

Donna's car was forced off the side of a steep canyon wall. Mark was thrown out of the car and survived, but Donna was trapped in the flaming wreckage and died in agony.

Shortly after that, Mark, Professor Haskins, and David Red Eagle took a pledge to bring Donna's killers to justice. In this case, justice for the Los Angeles mob came at the end of hot rifle slugs, .45 rounds, and a series of raids and bombing attacks that Mark used effectively, wiping out two-thirds of the large Los Angeles family and destroying the family's heroin pipeline. Mark came away from it with nearly half a million dollars in Mafia money. This was the first gangster "deposit" in the Penetrator's treasury to fight crime.

Since that time the Penetrator has challenged evil, madness, mobsters, and killers in almost every state of the union and in several overseas nations. He knows he can't live forever; some lucky shot or blow or knife will end his battle. But until that day comes he will keep on struggling against them all—from organized crime to the most refined white-collar criminals.

3

Chapter 1

HOT MEET ON A CHILLY DAY

Mark Hardin wrapped his hands around a heavy mug filled with hot coffee, trying to soak some of its warmth into his chilled fingers, but all the time he watched the electronics store across the street. The February cold had attacked his desert-thinned blood and nudged him inside the small cafe an hour ago.

He was not worried about being spotted. No one knew the Penetrator was in Chicago, and he had done little here to attract attention before. The thick moustache he had started his campaign with several years ago was now back in place. He reasoned that any current searchers would be looking for him without the face adornment. The Penetrator had also let his hair grow longer, so it could be styled and combed down to cover his ears in the sleek, Hollywood look that was now fading from favor. The two changes made a striking difference in the appearance of the big man. Large, tinted lensed glasses further shielded the Penetrator's identity.

He sipped the coffee, staring at the door of the

Bytes & Chips electronics store through the sifting of snow on the Chicago street. The snow had fallen two hours before, and now each passing car whirled and scattered it from one curb to the other.

This mission was getting more complicated by the hour. He had come to Chicago two days ago with the single purpose of tracking down the rumors that the giant Bainbridge Technical Corporation was in serious trouble and had been cheating its two million stockholders out of billions of dollars in legitimate dividends. If any skullduggery or manipulation were going on to cut the regular dividends and at the same time let corporate executives pocket huge bonuses and raises, Mark wanted to dig into the ripoff and stop it. At least a million "small fry" in the market held Bainbridge, one of the blue-chip traditionals. They were the little people who could ill afford the losses, and Mark was determined to check out the problem until he found the truth one way or the other.

The Penetrator went to the windy city under the cover name of H. Elrod Frost, a special investigating agent of the Internal Revenue Service reporting directly to the Washington, D.C., director's office.

He had received a frigid reception in the corporate offices at Bainbridge Technical and only the most minimal and grudging cooperation. A lack of profits meant fewer taxes, and if any fraud were involved, the tax people wanted to know about it. The cover story gave Mark access to parts of the corporate records he needed, but curiously, he found almost nothing to indicate any type of a major cover-up or ripoff. The profits simply had been shrinking, from $1.15 per share eighteen months ago to only twelve cents in this quarter.

Sliding profits are not unusual for any stock, but

5

Bainbridge Technical was a leader in the miniaturized computer field and should have been riding the crest of the surge with the other electronics giants such as Textronics, IBM, National Cash Register, Sony, and Texas Instruments. Rumors in the trade were that the problem was steadily antiquated management and a lack of flexibility.

In an industry where a six-month-old product might be out-dated and a liability, management had to be so quick and sharp it sometimes met corporate decisions bending back on themselves the same day. Top management at Bainbridge was Jethro Bainbridge, seventy-six, chairman of the board and chief operating officer. He had founded the company and done much of the early electronics inventing in the building years. Now he ruled with an iron fist, was almost never seen by the employees, and there were even reports that he had been dead for two years. He definitely was a Howard Hughes-type individual and one who wielded tremendous power.

But why the big drop in profits?

Once on the scene Mark found more complications. Bainbridge Technical had been almost entirely computerized four years ago. Its systems had programs laid over programs that served to function other programs, and it was regarded as the most highly computerized big business in the world. As such, it was made to order for electronic thefts and computer scams of every description by ingenious and bitter employees and former workers.

Electronic theft quickly became the firm's largest headache. There were many such stories in the file, but none of them seemed to add up to enough trouble to shake the foundations of a huge firm like Bainbridge. Then Mark found a familiar name in three separate reports. The individual was Duncan Danlow.

At twenty-five he was a genius in the computer field, but at thirty-five he was a graduate of Attica and Leavenworth. Danlow had been involved in an early electronic theft at Bainbridge. There hadn't been enough evidence to convict him. Evidently by now Danlow had learned a lot about electronically covering his tracks. Later Danlow was hired to advise the company how to safeguard a department and its products. A week after Danlow's consultations, the department was ripped off for over a hundred thousand dollars worth of valuable, easily sold computer parts. Again, Danlow was suspected, but there was not enough evidence even to bring charges.

Mark finished the coffee and watched two men leave the electronics store with large packages. The whole retail field of merchandising small business computers and now even home and hobby computers was still skyrocketing. Computer stores were mushrooming all over the nation.

The store he watched was evidently owned and operated by the same Duncan Danlow. Why was he running such a store when his natural instincts would be to use the computers for some kind of con game or outright theft? The coincidence of finding Danlow involved with the same company Mark was investigating was too much. Mark couldn't help but believe that there must be some connection, some tie-in, only so far he had found none. He'd try the direct approach. He'd checked earlier in the day only to find that Mr. Danlow was out but was expected back in about an hour. So far, two hours later, Mark had not seen him.

The Penetrator was about to signal for another cup of coffee when he changed his mind and instead put on his overcoat and went toward the door.

Mark Hardin was lean and fit like a professional

athlete in top condition. He was a large, powerful man, heavily muscled. His complexion was darker, than most, and his lingering suntan from California's desert accented it. He moved with the supple litheness of a stalking cougar. His dark eyes and taut face gave him a smoldering, troubled look. When he frowned, a deadly aura chilled those watching.

Mark kept his weight at two-hundred-five pounds with no effort. If he lost weight on a mission, he gained it back in a few days with little thought to diet. He had an NBC network newscaster accent, as American as possible, but close scrutiny might reveal a touch of a western twang to his speech.

As Mark paused at the cafe's door, he saw the man he had been waiting for uncoil from a car, wave the driver away, and turn into the electronics store. It was the same man Mark had seen in a dozen pictures, all six-feet-five inches of him. The man was built like a fishing pole without the line guides.

Mark edged into the stinging cold and hurried across the snow-slippery street towards the electronics store. Danlow had vanished inside moments before. As Mark stepped into the computer store, he did not see the owner. It was not a large place, twenty by forty perhaps, but jammed floor to ceiling with racks of computer components and small home computers ready to plug in and program. It was a haven for the do-it-yourself byte fan and electronics nut. There were racks of small business computers that five years ago took up two rooms of space and cost two hundred and fifty thousand dollars and now came in a pair of suitcase-type consoles for less than four thousand dollars.

Mark found the same clerk he had talked to before. "Is he here yet?"

The clerk was long-haired, under twenty-one, and

8

with thick-lensed glasses. He grinned. "Yeah, he just came in. Go on back, right through the door. The boss don't stand on being formal."

Mark hadn't even unbuttoned his overcoat. He went through the door into a small office with a desk, a chair and lamp, and a curious man who rose defensively.

Danlow was balding, wore glasses and a wool plaid shirt under a sports coat. He was also scowling.

"Yes?" Danlow asked cautiously.

"Danny Danlow. It's been a long time." Mark watched the man closely but spotted only a slight tightening around the corners of his eyes. He was surprised but tried not to show it.

"Sorry, I'm Ben Carlson. Who were you looking for?"

"Cut it out, Danlow. Attica, four years ago. I saw you in the yard all the time. Now and then in the library. Looks like you hit a good thing. You really own this place?"

Mark had moved close to the desk and now shot a stiff-fingered jab into Danlow's belly just under his rib cage. Danlow yelped in surprise and slumped in his chair, gasping for breath. Pain, then hatred, flooded his face, but when he looked up at Mark it was with considerably more respect.

"Who the hell are you?"

"You wouldn't remember me, Danlow. But I know you. There's too much action been going down around here lately. We know the computer hardware is coming from you. My boss wants it stopped."

"I don't know what you're talking about. I run a clean place. I got a license. The cops know about my record; so does the city and the feds. I'm clean. This place is legit. I sell components or complete computers to whoever has the cash or the credit."

9

"And you work on the side stealing companies blind with your computers. We know your scam, Danny. You just stay out of our territory, and we don't care." Mark leaned over the desk and patted down Danlow. "I didn't think you'd have a piece; you never did." Mark stared down at the man for a dozen seconds. "Danny, the boss says lay off his territory and his outfits, or he's gonna burn you down into one of them computers of yours and use you for glue. You read me, turkey?"

"Who's your boss?"

Mark grinned, then laughed. "Danny, Danny. You know better than that. You know who everybody works for or with in this end of town. I didn't even hear you say that." Mark's expression changed, and he reached over and grabbed the Pendleton wool shirt and pulled Danlow halfway out of the chair.

"Danlow, just don't you get too big for your goddamn britches, you read me, boy? You always did think you was too damn good for the rest of the guys in the joint. Well, we're not in the joint no more, Danlow, and we pay back old debts. You dig?" When the man didn't answer, Mark backhanded him across the face, slamming his head to one side.

"Yeah, I hear you," Danlow said through tight lips.

"You better, and hear good, Danlow, or you're dead." Mark turned and walked to the door, opened it, and without looking back went into the store.

Danlow touched his swelling right cheek tenderly, then grabbed the phone and dialed. The phone rang three times and Danlow pounded the desk in frustration as he waited.

At last it was picked up. "Wally? Yeah, it's me. Listen, no time to explain. He's big, about six-three, black overcoat, no hat, dark glasses, should be just about leaving my front door. Can you see him?"

There was a pause.

"Yeah, Danny, I've got him. Just coming out. Kind of a dark snake, like he's part Mex or something."

"That's the one. Two of you take him, break him up a little bit. I don't know who the hell he is, but he's trouble. He's a cocky son-of-a-bitch, so chop him down."

"Yeah, can do. No sweat, baby. I'll get back to you."

When Mark left the office, he moved around the store for a minute before he went outside. Why did he pick Chicago in February for fun and games? He buttoned up his overcoat and braved the swirling granules of snow. The Penetrator was taking his time, deliberately allowing someone to follow him if Danlow wanted them to. He didn't know what he might stir up here, but anything would be an improvement. He needed a lead, a handle, and he had come on tough to Danlow, hoping to spring some kind of action.

On the sidewalk Mark saw no one behind him. He crossed the street and checked out a store window, but again nothing moved that seemed directed at him. He was on the third window when he glanced behind and saw two men suddenly find a store display interesting. Mark moved on toward the corner. Once around the corner he sprinted down a lackluster street past two stores and dodged into the third doorway.

The snow changed to flakes and came down for a moment in a flurry. Mark edged toward the street and looked out the opening. The two men came around the corner slowly, and when they couldn't see Mark, they hurried.

Mark shrugged out of his overcoat and dropped it near the door behind him. There were few pedestri-

11

ans on this side street and mostly offices in the upper floors.

Mark stepped into the sidewalk a dozen feet ahead of the two striding thugs.

"You boys looking for me?" Mark asked.

One of them was five-ten and slender, the other heavier and as tall as Mark. They both stopped, shrugged, and looked at each other. They started to turn away, then in unison reversed their direction and charged straight at Mark. He let them come and at the last possible fraction of a second he jumped straight at them and jolted out both feet in a bent-knee kick to their chests. Both men tumbled backwards, and Mark dropped to the sidewalk on hands and feet, bouncing up quickly. He grabbed the smaller man and propelled him into the alley two doors down.

The larger man rolled to his feet, watched Mark a moment marching his buddy away, and ran down the street the other direction.

In the alley Mark slapped the smaller hoodlum and shook the dazed man.

"Okay, tough guy, who sent you to rough me up?"

"Huh?"

"Who sent you to beat me up?"

"Oh . . . Danny Danlow."

"Why? Who is he working with?"

"What? Working with? We work for Danny. Working with?" The expression, the sudden concern, the wonder, all pointed to an unmistakable character printout of a born follower who also seemed unusually confused. Mark had the idea the man might be slightly retarded as well. Mark pushed him against the wall and took out a chipped blue-flint arrowhead and gave it to the thug.

"Take this to your boss," Mark said. "And tell him I'm watching him. If he makes one false move, or if he gets just a little out of line, he'll wish he was never born."

The man blinked, evidently trying to remember the words. Mark turned and walked back to where he had left his overcoat and surprisingly found it still there.

So did he have a connection or didn't he? Danlow was afraid of somebody, and he kept a pair of low-grade thugs on his payroll. Mark didn't know why or how, but he was sure there was some tie-in between the big money loss by Bainbridge and the computer expert down the street. Now all he had to do was figure out the connection and what it meant.

Chapter 2

$15,000 THE EASY WAY!

Hector Lattimer made one final check on the suitcase open on the bed beside him. Yes, everything looked right. He had picked up the heavy case that morning and had spent two hours reading the instructions and looking over the schematic to mesh the new understanding with his basic knowledge of electronics and computer hardware.

Hector was thirty-six, an electronics engineer, now unemployed, on the slender side and five-feet-eight inches tall. Right now he was slightly overweight because of his tendency to eat when he was worried or anxious, and he had been both lately.

On the bed of his rented room sat a portable computer terminal. It was an Elliott with a built-in IBM Selectric typewriter printout and the necessary black boxes of electronic gear to turn an ordinary telephone into a direct contact with almost any computer in the country. The terminal was really little more than an extension of the telephone line to the automatic printout typewriter so the operator could talk back to the distant computer. The black boxes did all the work. The third component on the portable terminal was a depressed slot built into the case called a coupler where a regular telephone handset was inserted to complete the tie-in with the computer.

Hector studied the setup. He knew it would work. All he had to do was get a dial tone, put the phone into the coupler, and dial the special number to take him directly to a computer. Milliseconds later the machine would begin typing out word from the computer that it was ready for action.

Hector wiped a fringe of sweat beads off his forehead. He had waited so long for this day; he had hated Bainbridge and worked and prayed and hoped so much for this chance that it had to become a reality. Hector rubbed his balding forehead, adjusted his glasses, and sighed.

No he couldn't try it yet. First he had to get used to the idea that it was actually within his grasp. It had been three years now. Three years since the accident that had turned his right hand into a withered, immobile claw. He stared at it for a moment, then looked away.

Everyone said that electricity could do strange things. He had believed them since he worked with and around electricity all the time. But the blast of high voltage that had ripped through his hand on the way to a positive ground had not killed him. Everyone said the ten thousand volts should have fried him to a cinder. Many times he wished it had. Instead it had seared charred, and burned away much of the flesh on his right hand, destroyed nerves and cauterized capillaries, veins, and arteries.

For a year the company tried to figure out why he wasn't dead. He was a type of celebrity for a few weeks, but by the time his hand had been restruc-

15

tured with the remaining flesh, the skin grafts completed, and two fingers removed, the attention had dropped to nothing.

When he left the hospital after six months, no one noticed. He'd been married a short time, but his wife had left him years ago. There had been no children.

At last he reported back for his job at the set time, but found that he was shunted from one office to another. The answer was always the same. He simply was not physically able to perform the duties of a senior electronics engineer, an E-16, and there was no managerial engineering poisition open to him. So he was given involuntary medical retirement and received retirement pay, insurance, and industrial compensation. He would get it all for the rest of his life. But was that really a life?

The new mental shock of being thrown out of his job was almost as hard as losing his hand. Not even an appeal directly to Mr. Bainbridge himself had done any good. The company president had visited Hector's bedside in the hospital that first week and said any man who could fight off ten thousand volts of electricity would have a job at Bainbridge Technical for as long as he wanted one.

Lattimer blinked back the beginnings of moisture in his green eyes and stared down at the computer terminal. All he had to do was dial the number.

He plugged the terminal into the wall socket, picked up the phone, and listened to the steady dial tone. Hector put the phone into the coupler slot in the suitcase. Then he dialed precisely the special seven-digit number that would put him into direct touch with the bank's computer.

He couldn't hear it ring, but he knew it must have, and a moment later the typewriter in the case began clicking out words on the continuous 8½-by-11-inch fanfold paper, with two carbons.

"SIGN ON."

Hector nodded. This was normal computer procedure. He typed in the special identification key.

"CA-7731."

"CA-7731. CUSTOMER ACCOUNTS, REQUIRES SECONDARY KEY CLEARANCE."

Again Hector looked at his notes and typed in a second number.

"CA-1310."

Almost at once the computer responded.

"WHAT PROCESS?"

"Begin Process 414."

"PROCESS 414 FOR WHAT ACCOUNT?"

"Account 010-4184."

"BEGIN PROCESS 414 FOR ACCOUNT 010-4184. WHAT TRANSACTION? 1. EXTEND CREDIT LINE. 2. REDUCE CREDIT LINE. 3. HOLD ALL BALANCE IN ACCOUNT. 4 RELEASE BALANCE FOR PAYOUTS."

"Transaction Code desired, 1."

"WHAT AMOUNT EXTENSION?"

"Extend to $15,000."

"EXTEND TO $15,000 CREDIT LINE ACCOUNT 010-4184."

The machine remained quiet for a few seconds. Hector felt sweat dripping off his eyebrows, staining his underarms. What was taking so long? These things functioned in a millionth of a second. The machine chattered again.

"PROCESS COMPLETE ON ACCOUNT 010-4184."

"WHAT PROCESS?"

The computer was asking Hector for another job.

He looked at his notes and quickly typed in new instructions:

"Begin Process 515."

"PROCESS 515 FOR WHAT ACCOUNT?"

"Account 010-4184."

"BEGIN PROCESS 515 FOR ACCOUNT 010-4184. WHAT TRANSACTION? 1. CHECK BALANCE. 2. CREDIT BALANCE. 3. DEBIT BALANCE."

"Transaction Code desired, 2."

"CREDIT WHAT FIGURE?"

"Credit $15,000 this date."

"CREDIT $15,000, ACCOUNT 010-4184."

Again there was a momentary pause as the computer did its work.

"PROCESS COMPLETE ON ACCOUNT 010-4181."

It dropped down two lines on the machine then:

"WHAT PROCESS?"

The machine was ready for more instructions. Hector gave a whoop of joy and stared again at the printout. He had done it! He had just stolen $15,000 by computer. Now all he had to do was go to the bank and pick up the money. He looked at the terminal. He should shut it down. Quickly he typed in: "Process complete." Then he took the phone from the coupler and hung it up. Now there was no way he could be traced. For a moment he thought about going back into the computer and using the special maintenance procedures to call up the transactions log and reprogram it to take off any record of the dealings on account 010-4184, but he decided he didn't need that kind of protection on this one. Not if he acted quickly and picked up the money before anyone discovered the spurious deposit.

Hector sat down and let the sweep of emotion surge over him. Tears came to his eyes. He rememered the long months in the hospital. The pain, the terrified looks even now when children saw his hand, the shudders of pretty women, and the pity of some of the men.

He had refused the medical people's offer of a mechanical hand. He didn't want to be half machine. What was left of him had to be all real, even if it didn't work.

The bank—he had to get there before three. He turned off the terminal and put the top on it; he dressed in his best suit, the dark blue with a pinstripe. He shaved carefully with his electric razor, which he could manipulate better left-handed than he could a blade, and combed what was left of his hair. Then, satisfiied that he looked like a successful businessman, he sat at the small dresser and wrote a check to "cash" for $14,900 and signed it with the name of that account, Leonard Wilcoxen.

Lattimer got out of the cab in front of the Midwestern National Trust Bank ten minutes before closing time. He stood in the line inside that served all the tellers, and drew the window of a pretty young girl of about twenty. She looked at the amount of the check, smiled, and said she'd have to check with her supervisor. She went to the operations officer, who glanced at the check, looked at Lattimer, and punched several buttons on a foot-square video screen in front of her. Hector imagined that it was a computer video display for checking balances. He could almost see the viewerscreen popping up with the balance in the account of $15,000. A moment later the smiling girl came back.

"Sir, I'll have to go to the vault for the money if you want it in cash. Perhaps you could use a cashier's check."

"No, miss, I need the money. Make it all in hundreds, please, new bills if you have them."

She nodded and went to the supervisor again. It took the girl and the other woman over five minutes to get the bills from the vault, and then to have another teller double count the amount of cash. At the window the girl carefully counted out the hundreds again in stacks of ten. She came out correctly with nine bills in the last stack. Then she put the money in an envelope with a rubber band around it.

"Thank you, Mr. Wilcoxen, and please come back again," she said.

He looked at the envelope. It made a remarkably small package. A hundred and forty-nine bills, all new, crisp and beautiful. A stack not an inch thick.

He put the envelope in his inside jacket pocket and walked out of the bank. It had taken so long, so very long. Outside he wanted to scream for joy but knew that he couldn't. It would wait until he got home.

His mind quickly turned to the practical, the engineer thinking again. He still owed $500 on the portable terminal. And he had promised ten percent of anything he earned with it to the seller. He would have to pay, because Danny would know—he'd find out. So Hector would pay. He'd give Danny a thousand. But he wouldn't tell Danny anything about any other action he had coming up. The big one, that's what he was excited about now. This had been only a test run, a scrimmage to see how the real game would go. The big one would strike at the heart, the brain, of the corporation and hurt it badly.

But he still needed the access numbers. The two words bored a hole in his head. He had everything he needed now axcept the new access numbers. But he would get them. He had a plan, and what was more important, he had a source.

The bank account in the Wilcoxen name at Midwestern would soon be closed. It had been opened three months before with a hundred dollars as a blind, as one place to deposit money. He had several of them near his room. But even so, a fake account used once was dead. It was too easy to trace. And the automatic cameras might be used on all big withdrawals, he wasn't sure.

Now to the matter at hand. Those damned access numbers. Those key numbers the computer demanded. They were the clues to his either becoming a multimillionaire or trying to live forever by upgrading fake bank accounts with the ready reserve line of credit scam. None of that. He would get the numbers, and he would be a millionaire!

Chapter 3

A GREEN-EYED PROBLEM

Mark Hardin sat in the private office of an attractive young woman named Barbara Simpson. She was listed as the Director of Computer Program Application. Mark had introduced himself under his cover name as an IRS investigator and was dressed appropriately. He wore a conservative three-piece soft gray business suit with a gold chain across the vest pocket and on one end of the chain a traditional gold watch.

The girl eyed him coolly. He guessed she was twenty-five or -six.

"I thought I had made that ultimately clear, Mr. Frost. I am the corporate computer program application director here at Bainbridge Technical. Yes, you are quite correct. On some material even the corporate vice presidents look to me for advice, and in a few matters I can and do overrule a vice president. I fail to see how you can be confused about the scope of my duties."

When she stood, she was shorter than he had expected as he had entered her office a dozen minutes ago. She was dressed in a low-key elegance that Mark recognized as being deceptively expensive. Her jewelry was in good taste: a gold pin near her left shoulder and two large gold and diamond rings on her right hand. But what interested him most was the way she held her head and shoulders—the ultimate in detached reserve. Framing an oval face and high cheekbones that looked slightly Indian, her hair was a light brown—untinted, he decided—but stylishly cut for minimum care. Her best feature was her eyes, luminous light green that fascinated him and made him stammer for the first time since the seventh grade when Jody Bennet had kissed him in front of the whole class.

"That was corporate computer program application director," Mark said to fill in the gap he had left as he watched her. "And you report directly to Jethro Bainbridge himself, the president of the firm?"

"That's correct. Computer logic, programming, organization, overhead planning, and applications have a language all their own. For example, if I said I wanted a small computer that has an LSI-11 CPU, a 4096 x 16 read/write MOS semiconductor memory, DMA operation and executes the PDP-11-40 instructions, would you have any idea what I was talking about?"

Mark chuckled. She was good. "No, of course not. I'm an accountant, not an electronics expert. I understand your point, Miss Simpson. I'm only questioning the organizational structure that puts a computer application director in decision-making levels above corporate vice presidents." He held up his hand to stop her protest. "I can question it without requiring any accountability, accountingwise."

Her green eyes never left his. "I understand that for the past two days you've been spreading absolute havoc among our people in accounting. Of course you realize that everything done there first goes through banks of computers to align, systematize, channel, and categorize the information into proper accounting reference and report areas. Much of the evaluation and printout work is also handled on programs with little human input. The final evaluations on program projections, naturally, are done by human account and departmental evaluators."

"Well, yes, Miss Simpson. But what surprised me was that it took me a day and a half to get to your office, to find a place where I could get some real answers. I wonder why that was?" She only smiled at him without responding. "At least I've come to the right spot now. Maybe we can get started so I can do my job. One point in which my department is interested is the vulnerability of such a total computer system to electronic theft—and we have a string of half a dozen such thefts, duly claimed as deductions by your firm, that we are decidedly anxious to explore. Had you considered such thefts when you went ahead with the total computerization of your company?"

She nodded, and for the first time he saw the edge of a smile touch her pretty face. She deliberately licked her lips as if anticipating a pleasant task.

"Mr. Frost. Picture a dozen floors on a building this size with a thousand accountants on each floor. Multiply this times fifty firms around the world. That's a lot of accountants entering figures on a lot of ledger sheets.

"Two floors below I have three small rooms that daily do the work of those 600,000 accountants we talked about. The computers do the work faster, without mistakes, and they never get hay fever, never get ill, don't need time off to get married or take a vacation—and they never get pregnant. The computers do

24

the accounting a hundred times faster and better than accountants ever could."

Mark stood and walked to the side of the room to the expensively draped double windows that looked out over Lake Michigan.

"You set me up for that one, Miss Simpson, and you scored a point. But are you saying that you *tolerate* computer theft because, even with it, you're money ahead in the long run?"

"We tolerate no theft. Every case has been investigated, seven have resulted in convictions, three were found to be not theft but simple human errors in programming. We currently have three cases under investigation."

"Including one for over $115,000 from two weeks ago?"

"Yes, including that one, Mr. Frost. How does this have anything to do with the Internal Revenue Service?"

"A theft becomes deductible, Miss Simpson, as I'm sure you know. So are computers, programmers, programs, all the trappings of the computer world. So we are vitally interested. Feeding a computer is deductible; feeding an accountant isn't. We're interested in every aspect of profit/loss procedures."

She stood, walked across the office, and snapped off the soft music that had been flooding gently through the carpeted room. She moved with the liquid grace of a ballet dancer. "Mr. Frost, I find all this a little hard to believe. You're harrassing us, and I don't know why. I called the local IRS office, and they don't know you. I called the regional office, and they said they handle the bookkeeping only and not complaints or investigations. They did tell me that if you came from the Washington office they wouldn't know you. But they said it was usual routine for Washington to notify them of something like an investigation such as this. So I think you're here just to cause us trouble." Part of her reserve slipped, and she frowned at him.

"Miss Simpson, I can show you detailed police reports that indicate that Bainbridge Technical has lost more than $340,000 through computer theft and fraud in the past two years. I came here to try to learn more about how this type of crime takes place and to try to devise some methods or procedures to help you stop it. We had hoped you would give us your full cooperation. Instead, I show my card, and the whole office goes into a panic, and it takes me two days to find out to whom I should talk. We are not in the process of contesting your company's tax returns or in auditing your books. We're trying to tie down some procedures to prevent computer theft so we can advise other businesses on plans to help them stop such thefts. I'm an investigator trying to gather the facts, build up specific case studies, and with your help, make some recommendations as to how the thefts might be stopped."

Barbara Simpson stood, lit a cigarette, and at once stubbed it out. "I'm trying to quit," she said. She walked to the window and back to her chair. "You're not really after us, trying to accuse us of something?"

"No."

"So we don't have to be afraid of you?"

"Not for any reason."

"Well, at least that's a relief. I'm not programmed for this high-pressure governmental threat world." She lit another cigarette, and when Mark held up one finger accusingly, she stubbed the smoke out. "Right, really. I know I should quit." She sighed and looked out the window. "I came here as a programmer consultant five years ago. Since then I've built up the computer program utilization here much more completely than I ever dreamed we could. Mr. Bainbridge liked my work and helped me expand it. Now we are one of the biggest departments in the whole corporate office and one of the most important. The thefts seemed to be a natural outgrowth of the advances. Like a farmer losing a few apples to the kids who live next door to his orchard. But I'm a computer person, and I don't do well with all the damn people problems."

"Like the people who use your computers to steal from you?"

"Those and others. Yes, I admit that we've had our share of computer crimes. More than you know about, but we don't need any more bad publicity about it." She stared at him over frowning green eyes. "Are you really an IRS snoop? You don't look like any of the others we've had in here. You look more like an athlete, maybe a decathlon champ."

"Sorry, but it's my job to dig into this computer crime."

"How about a small free-lance job on the side? I've got another problem that you could help me with."

"What kind of problem?"

She looked at the clock on her desk. "Why don't we talk about it over dinner? My apartment is just down the hall, and I hate to eat alone. Please come."

"Miss Simpson, I don't like to eat alone either. I'd be pleased to come."

She smiled, and her features took on a soft glow accented by those glittering green eyes that fascinated Mark.

"This way," she said, moving out from the large irregularly shaped desk. They went through a door into a conference room, with executive-type, high-backed soft swivel chairs clustered around a walnut table. They went into the hall and through two more locked doors before she ushered him into an elegantly furnished living room. It was sunken three steps on one side and faced a window wall eight feet tall and thirty feet wide that looked across Lake Michigan and a million lights that had come on in the winter dusk. The scene was breathtaking.

"Do you like it?" she asked smiling gently.

"It's fantastic, beautiful."

"I sit here sometimes just watching the changing lights. The company owns it, of course. It's part of my salary. Now, would you like a drink before dinner?"

He nodded, trying to figure how a hired hand would rate an executive apartment like this in a deluxe office building where space was at a premium and expensive. Something like this would rent for $3,000 a month on the open market.

She brought him a glass of wine.

"That's a special chablis; I think you'll like it." They sat on a deep, soft couch that faced the window wall.

"You said something about another problem that tied in. I need to know everything about your computer crime situation."

"I'm not sure about this one yet. It may only be a wild threat, but it's something that does concern me." She moved on the couch and leaned back, watching the lights far below. Mark was strongly aware of the effect she had on him, and he didn't try to fight it.

"Why don't you quit the IRS and come to work for Bainbridge? We always need investigators in one area or another."

"Sorry, I like what I do, and I have a lot of freedom. Now, what about this other matter?"

She brought a tape recorder from a bookcase and pushed the play button. At once a slightly wheezing voice came on, and to Mark's practiced ear the sound had that quality that often comes when a person is faking a special sound. It was not the man's real voice. Mark listened attentively.

"This is a special message for Bainbridge Technical Corporation. Listen carefully, you big shots! Listen and realize that I am sincere, that I'm not some crackpot or kook. I mean every word that I say. I am in a position to withdraw from the Bainbridge firm a million dollars a day anytime I want to. I have the plans, the technology. But I am willing to refrain from going to all this work if you will pay me five million dollars at once in used fifty and hundred dollar bills. I will indicate to you later where and how the money will be picked up.

"Remember, I am sincere and dedicated. I can do what I say I can do. This cassette will not self-destruct, although I could have made it do so. Rather I want you to keep it and study what I say and how I say it. Five million dollars. Get it ready for later delivery. I'll be in contact with you."

The tape ended, and Mark looked up at the luminous green eyes that watched him.

"How does this tie in with your computers?"

"He said 'withdraw' in the tape. At least half of our computer thefts were transacted by going through the bank and utlizing our computer codes for automatic withdrawls and transfers of funds. I think this is what he's talking about, this type of a withdrawal. But is he sincere? Will he and can he do what he suggests?"

"It was a false voice, but it had that quality, that ring, of truth to it. I would say you have a serious problem here." Mark watched her losing her composure. Her chin quivered for a second, she blinked, and a moment later she crumpled against his shoul-

29

der. Tears flowed down her cheeks; quiet sobs shook her slender body. Barbara's wet eyes stared at him.

"I . . . I just don't know what to do. I've had some hard decisions in the past, but this is the worst thing I've ever faced." She put her head back on his shoulder and sobbed.

Mark had no thoughts that this was an act for his benefit. She didn't know his line of work, so she could gain nothing by any playacting here. One point bothered Mark.

"Miss Simpson, I can't understand how this could possibly be your responsibility. It seems this would be the board of directors' task, or the chairman of the boards, at least. Why are you handling it?"

She leaned away from him and sat up, wiping wetness from her eyes, smearing some of her eye makeup.

"Well, they . . . they gave me the job. Told me to take care of it. They thought it was a joke and said they couldn't be bothered." She gulped for breath to keep another sob stilled. She looked up at him. "You think he means it? The extortionist?"

"Yes, I think so. And that interests me, especially if it's going to be a computer crime."

"But why the IRS?" she asked, calming a little. "Why are you people interested in it?"

"Miss Simpson. Anytime anyone shows a big business loss, an unusually heavy loss, we're especially interested. Sometimes it means that a business is manipulating costs, profits, and liabilities to avoid paying its fair share of taxes. Then the little guys, the millions of wage earners, have to dig down deeper to pay their own share of taxes as well as those the giant corporation that has cheated its way out of. I don't like that kind of game, I won't play it, and I hope that Bainbridge Technical won't play that game either."

She had regained some of her composure now. Barbara Simpson wiped her eyes carefully and turned to him. "So what are we going to do about the extortionist? How can we tell if he's really a threat?"

A chime rang, and Barbara rose gracefully, apologized, and went into the hall to a door. The voices were loud, and Mark could hear the conversation. Part of it came on a speaker set inside the door.

"Miss Simpson, this is Roscoe Bainbridge, I demand to see my father. If you don't let me in to see him, I'll have you fired!"

"Now, Mr. Bainbridge, of course you can come in. You know that your father has been ill, and he's under sedation. Right now he couldn't talk to you even if you did go in to see him, so what's the use? You tell me what you want, and I'll get to him first thing in the morning when he wakes up."

There was a short pause, and Mark heard the intercom click on.

"Dammit to hell, Simpson! That's the same line you gave me last time, and three times before that. I haven't seen the old man for three months now. At least let me in and talk with you."

"Of course, Mr. Bainbridge. There, the door's open, come in."

Mark moved to the side of the room where he could see into the hall. Roscoe Bainbridge was nearly fifty, balding, twenty pounds overweight, and dressed like a country squire. He had all the trappings and mannerisms of a rich spoiled brat grown to middle age.

"It's about time you opened the door, young lady. Now take me to my father at once." Bainbridge held a small caliber automatic in his right hand.

Mark sauntered into the hall as if nothing had happened. He was watching the girl, ignoring the man with the gun.

"Barbara what's the idea of asking another man to the apartment? You said tonight was my night. I'm furious with you, Barbara!" As he talked, he moved toward them but turned so he could see only Barbara. The man with the gun was so surprised that he did little more than watch.

Mark put his hands on his hips in apparent anger.

"Look, woman, you want to entertain other men, fine, just tell me so I'm not here." Mark turned toward Roscoe Bainbridge. The men stood only four feet apart. The gun now swung to point at Mark.

"Don't move," Bainbridge said.

Mark looked down for the first time as if just noticing the gun. "A toy pistol, how droll. I suppose you don't even know that the safety is still on."

Bainbridge looked down.

Mark sprang forward, his right hand rising and chopping down on Bainbridge's wrist. The movement came so suddenly, so quickly, that the older man didn't have time to get off a shot. Mark eased the blow just enough so it wouldn't break the wrist, then hit him and sent the gun dropping to the carpeted floor. Mark kicked it away and picked it up. He worked the slide. The weapon was not loaded.

Five minutes later Barbara had calmed down Roscoe Bainbridge, made him a margarita, and explained again that she simply couldn't take him in to see his father.

"The doctor gave me strict orders about his nights. When he's under sedation, he's sleeping, but he still realizes when someone new comes in. It disturbs him, and he can't sleep well for days. Give me the proposal you wanted to show him, and I'll get it on his tray first thing tomorrow morning. I'll phone you in Midland before the day is over. Won't that work out all right?"

"I still think you've been giving me the runaround. I still think he's sicker than you're telling me. Hell, he could be dead for all I know."

"Well he's not, and you can count on that. He's pleased the way you're taking more interest in running Michigan Associates. Your plant is turning out the components now at a better rate than ever before. He's pleased. He also told me to congratulate you on that New York to Bermuda race. Didn't you come in second in your class?"

"No, third, but I had a crew problem. It was my best race ever. If I just had a better boat. Maybe a ten meter."

"Mr. Bainbridge, why don't you leave the proposal with me, and I'll get it to your father tomorrow."

"Yes, all right." He looked broken, defeated again. "I guess so. It doesn't really matter anyway. Damn!" He stood and headed for the door but stopped near Mark. "I've never seen anybody move so fast before. Are you one of those karate guys?"

Mark shook his head, and Bainbridge walked on by.

A few moments later Barbara Simpson came back. She slumped into the couch near Mark and looked at him through hooded eyes.

"I don't know what I would have done if you hadn't been here. I mean that gun! I'm terrified of guns. I would have done anything he told me to."

"Roscoe is the prodigal son?"

"More than that, but he's calmed down in the last few years. He's the sole heir to the Bainbridge fortune. He's generally not the violent type, and he's weak, introverted, and a really bad businessman. Once in a while he slips out of Michigan and comes to town. He has three VPs there who run the business and let him think he does. He spends most of his time sailing boats in long ocean races."

"And the old man would just as soon forget all about his son?"

"Something like that."

"How come he came here? Are you the real power behind the throne? This certainly has nothing to do with computers."

She sighed, watched him steadily. "Mr. Frost, that's really none of your business, is it? Now, what about this extortion threat? If you can help me with it, I'll pay you well. Is it real?"

"I'd say that it is. But that all depends whether you hear from the man again or not."

"What if he doesn't contact us again?"

"Home free, I'd say. Unless he steals you blind."

A telephone chimed a four-note tune. Barbara got up slowly and answered it where it rested in a small alcove.

"Yes?" she said, then listened, her eyes going wide. She pushed a button on the phone, and the same voice Mark had heard on the tape casette boomed into the room.

". . . that this is to convince you that I know what I am doing. I'll give you the telephone access numbers and code checks to gain entry into the bank computer, which can then transfer money from that series of Bainbridge accounts to any bank or account I specify. Are you listening, Miss Simpson?"

"Yes, but how did you get this number?"

"The same way I got the code numbers. I have planned carefully, thoroughly, and I will not be stopped nor caught. The number for the computer at the Johnston Street First City Bank where Bainbridge has its personnel retirement account is 363-1111.

34

This puts me into touch with the computer. Then the access key to the retirement funds is KX 0407. At that point the computer asks me for the classified second key number which is 7011. I hope you wrote down those numbers so you can check them."

"Yes, I did. I'm amazed that you know all this. I don't have my code and key book with me, but you can be sure I'll check those numbers, and if you are correct, they will be changed at once. Most of our key codes will be changed."

"That's fine, because I'll get the new ones and then I'll steal a million a day from you, and you won't know who did it or exactly how. To prevent that I now demand ten million dollars. I want you to send it by Bankwire II through the Europa Bankwire computer intertie to the Lausanne Bank of Switzerland, account 021-1264-2121. Your deposit must be made within twenty-hour hours, or your firm will suffer its first tragic loss. And I mean a loss besides the money. It will all be activated and operated through your massive computer system!"

The caller hung up abruptly and the unused line hummed through the room's telephone speaker.

Barbara put down the phone and turned to Mark, her lovely face streaked with new tears, her lower lip quivering. She ran to the next room and unlocked a drawer from a small desk and looked for a sheaf of papers. They were at the top of the third drawer.

"The key numbers he gave, those are the correct numbers! The caller can do it! He can order money out of any of the retirement accounts!" She looked at Mark and the tears came faster, her shoulders slumped. For a moment it seemed that she might fall. Then she straightened. "What in the world am I going to do?"

Chapter 4

DEADLY CHANCE ENCOUNTER

Barbara Simpson lost the confused, frightened expression she had worn during the phone call from the extortionist. She turned to Mark with determination showing on her pretty face.

"I'm sorry, Mr. Frost, but I'll have to give you a rain check on that dinner I promised. Suddenly I have a mass of work that must be done quickly. I hope you won't mind."

"Changing those key numbers for the computer?"

"Exactly. All of them in the retirement accounts. We couldn't change all of the others. He probably only knows the retirement codes."

"And I can't help?"

"No, you can't. I'm starting a much stricter security procedure with the confirmation check numbers now." She walked toward the door, and he followed.

As he went out of the apartment, she touched his arm. "I didn't mean to be so abrupt and discourteous. I hope we can arrange our dinner date for later."

"Don't worry; I'll give you a call tomorrow."

She smiled and closed the door.

Mark had never been attracted to pushy, dominant females, but then the clinging vine, 1940s model wasn't his favorite either. He had several items to check out before he could think about dinner with Barbara Simpson, especially if she didn't cooperate better on the phone than she had so far.

Mark touched the elevator button on the thirty-second floor and entered automatically when it stopped. No one else was on board. He rode to the ground floor and went out the front door. The guard nodded to him. In two minutes it would be six o'clock, and then everyone would have to sign in and out of the building. Mark had just left the Bainbridge Tower's big double doors and gone down three steps toward the sidewalk when a slender young man about five-ten walked toward him intentionally. The man's eyes caught Mark's, and the stranger held up his hand.

"Sir, could I talk to you for a moment? Someone said you dropped your wallet. Is this yours?" He held up a billfold that was well-worn, crushed to the shape of someone's pocket.

Mark shook his head, wondering what the gimmick was, the come on. But the man said nothing more. The wind blew a few flakes of new snow around them. The air was colder now.

"No, that isn't my wallet," Mark said. "Mine isn't that style, and it's safely buttoned in my pocket."

As he spoke, Mark saw the fires of hatred spring into the man's eyes. Smoothly the man moved beside Mark, and now Mark saw the newspaper over his arm. The Penetrator guessed there was a gun under the paper, but he felt no fear, only curiosity. Who was this man, and what did he want?

The man pushed the paper against Mark's side, and the muzzle of a weapon pressed into his ribs. It would be easy to crush the man and disarm him on the spot in front of Bainbridge Tower. But that would leave too many questions unanswered. How had this man known that Mark was here? Why was he waiting for Mark to come out? Had the gunman made a mistake? Was this just a robbery attempt, or was the stranger actually after the Penetrator? A shot in this crowded area could injure or kill some innocent bystander.

"You son of a bitch!" It was obvious the young man was trying to hold in his pent-up fury, his rage. "I never dreamed I'd ever find you. This is a gun in your ribs, and you're not fast enough to beat a bullet, so don't try any of your fancy stuff. I know what you did in Seattle. So just stay calm and stay alive."

"I think you're making a mistake," Mark said.

"You made the mistake, you bastard. I should shoot you down right here, but too many people would see me."

His eyes darted one way, then the other. Dozens of people were coming and going on the sidewalk, rushing for transport, looking for taxis. The falling snow came heavier now.

"I saw you come into the building this afternoon, and I thought it was you. But I had to hear your voice to be positive. You talked to my brother before you killed him in Seattle. You probably don't even remember his name. It was Dominic Scolari, and he was a hell of a good cop. You never gave him a chance. So I'm not giving you a chance."

"I never argue with a gun," Mark said.

"Then move down this way and walk carefully, or this .45 will blow your heart into pieces. I waited until most of the people had left the building and thought I'd missed you. But I went right on waiting,

38

even outside in the cold. It was a billion to one chance that I'd ever see you again, but here you are."

They walked down the sidewalk, side by side. Mark let the man dictate the direction. They left the heavily traveled street and turned into a less busy one; then abruptly the man pointed Mark into a store entrance fifteen feet deep and six feet wide. The store was closed.

The thin young man angled Mark into the entranceway and stepped back, his face again showing his hatred. "You not only gunned down my brother; you involved him in a theft ring. You blackened his reputation and his memory, and for that I'll never forgive you."

Mark remembered—the Seattle crooked police ring of thieves and the cop killers who hired out to the Seattle Mafia. A whole rotten barrel.

"Your brother was in a theft ring and was a killer, Scolari. He had a chance to give up and chose not to. He called the shots on his own funeral."

Mark slapped the gun away from the man so quickly Scolari never saw his hand move. Suddenly the .45 spun through the air and clattered on the cement. Scolari had seemed to expect to lose the weapon. At once he pulled two switchblade knives from his pockets and snicked them open, holding one in each hand in a knife-fighting pose that told Mark that the man was an expert with the blades.

"How are you against cold steel, big man?" Scolari asked.

Mark had no intention of drawing his own .45. The man made a feint, then slashed, and the Penetrator saw that Scolari was accomplished with the knives. Mark did not consciously remember the first law of unarmed self-defense: Cut down your attacker's mobility. But he did just that quickly and automatically.

The Penetrator's hard-soled shoe shot out in a short, hard kick that slammed into the knifeman's right knee, jolting it sideways, dislocating the knee joint from its socket. It was a simple, nonlethal attack Mark had used many times before to put down a troublesome opponent he didn't want to kill.

Scolari staggered but maintained his feet. The pain was horrendous in the disjointed knee. Mark had felt the same thing himself.

"You bastard!" Scolari roared. "I'll still get you!" Scolari's arm went back and whipped forward. Mark saw the knife coming from close quarters. It was a no-spin throw. Mark saw the movement, judged its course and leaped away. The blade whispered past his chest, and Mark drove in, kicking at the attacker's other leg. He contacted it and sent Scolari tumbling to the concrete floor of the entranceway.

Mark leaped back, ready for the next attack, but Scolari didn't rise. He didn't even move. Mark approached the downed man cautiously, using his foot to roll over the crumpled form.

The man's second knife had caught him as he fell and pierced his chest and slashed through his heart. Another Scolari was dead.

That was when Mark remembered how Sergeant Dominic Scolari also had liked to use a knife, how he had murdered the guard at the furrier in Seattle so his buddies could steal a truckload of valuable fur coats.

The Italian family must have had tremendously strong ties to produce so much hatred and revenge. But this was only a chance meeting, one in a billion. Mark didn't have to worry about any Scolari family concentrated search.

From the street light glow of the front of the building a man looked in, curious. "Hey, that guy hurt? What happened in there?"

Mark looked over his shoulder at the middle-aged man with glasses. In the dark of early evening, Mark knew the man had seen little of the attack, perhaps none.

"I think this man had a heart attack. You better run and call the police and an ambulance," Mark said.

"Yes, yes. There's a phone down on the corner," the man said and hurried in that direction.

Mark made sure his messenger had vanished, and then the Penetrator went to the sidewalk and walked in the opposite direction through the frosting of fresh snow. Two minutes later he was lost among the other pedestrians bundled against the cold, hurrying toward home and family and a warm fire.

The Penetrator shut the incident out of his mind. It was a chance happening. He had long ago resolved not to worry about such incidents, to take care of each situation as it developed, and then to forget about it. He could not afford to worry about something over which he had no control. If he did, he would be paranoid in a week.

He had enough problems here without any added ones. The project must come first. He turned back toward his hotel, watching another shower of dry snow falling, drifting and swirling through the tall buildings, whipped by capricious wind currents until some of the flakes made it to the street.

Mark went to his room in the Capitol Hotel and checked the door. It had not been opened since he left. Inside, nothing had been disturbed. He ordered dinner sent up, a blood-rare-steak, and concentrated on the tasks he had to do before morning.

Chapter 5

LOVE CONQUERS ALL, TELLS ALL

Hector Lattimer left the phone booth with a satisfied, frigid smile that matched the February weather. He had just finished a call to Bainbridge Technical and had talked with Miss Barbara Simpson, the head co-ordinator for the firm's computer programs. He had given her the ten-million-dollar demand and the sample code check numbers for the computer access to one of the Bainbridge accounts. She had almost panicked; he had felt it. By now she must know for certain that he meant business. He walked down the street slowly through the light shower of cold, dry snow.

He was heading for a slightly more enjoyable task. Her name was Iris McGrew, and she was about thirty, unmarried, and held an important position with the Lake Commercial Trust Bank of Chicago, where Bainbridge Technical had most of its corporate transfer accounts. It was a bank catering mainly to large business firms. Iris McGrew was one of the monitors of some of the largest firms, dealing closely with the customers, and arranging for code and key clearances with the companies on their accounts for Bankwire II and other computer deposits, withdrawals, and transfers of huge amounts of corporate funds from one subsidiary or banch to another. She wore only lipstick as a cosmetic, and her face was what the most doting mother would call "interesting" but never pretty.

It had taken him two months to meet and cultivate Iris. Twice they had gone to concerts, which Iris loved. Three times he had taken her to dinner, and only on the last date, two days ago, had he kissed her. It had been a slow-building process.

Iris McGraw was not a girlish romantic. She stood five-five and weighed about a hundred and forty pounds. Her black hair was styled ten years behind the times, and her clothes were simple packaging to cover her body with little effort at style or grace.

None of this deterred Hector. She was simply business, and that was a matter of logic and performance. He carried a bottle of champagne and a box of assorted soft cream chocolates that were Iris' favorites. The champagne would be a surprise and the key to the evening's work.

Iris lived in an apartment on an unimpressive block at small buildings a half mile from the Loop. When he rang her bell, she buzzed the downstairs door for him without question, and he hurried inside out of the freezing cold.

A few moments later he knocked on her apartment door, and when it opened, Hector thought for a moment he was at the wrong place. But the girl was Iris. She had been to a beauty parlor and had her hair cut shorter and set into some kind of a frothy whirl. She wore a touch of eye makeup and pale lipstick and looked almost pretty. He went wide-eyed as he knew she would expect him to do.

"Iris, you fixed your hair. It looks marvelous! Yes, indeed, what a pretty girl you are tonight! Isn't that a new dress, too?"

It had cost her forty-five dollars and was tight and slinky, but if it worked, it was more than worth it. She moved now and felt embarrassed at the way her breasts swayed and bounced under the low-cut top of the dress. Judy, her one true friend at work and her mentor for this big occasion, had insisted that Iris not wear a bra tonight. It was the first time ever that Iris hadn't worn a bra in public or with a man around. She smiled nervously and nodded to his question about the dress.

"You look simply marvelous! This is a cause for a celebration." Hector leaned out and kissed her softly on the lips. She held there a moment in sweet rapture as he pulled back. "Hello, pretty girl. How is our dinner coming?"

It broke the spell, and she laughed nervously and turned sharply, glad he couldn't see the way her breasts swung and bounced. She would never go without a bra again!

She had the dinner ready, steaks medium rare, with peas, potatoes, and small white onions in a cheese sauce, with side dishes of carrots and broccoli. For dessert there was layer cake and ice cream.

"Wow, that was some dinner," he said as he finished eating and pushed away from the table.

She reached out and held his hand. He had told her his name was Harry Anderson and he was in the real estate business.

"Harry, I think this is the most wonderful evening of my whole life," she said, her eyes brimming with affection.

44

He lifted her hand and kissed it. "Sweet Iris, this is only the beginning. Only the start of years of good days together."

After dinner they moved into the small living room and sat on the couch. He put his arm around her, and she snuggled against him. He talked about the stock market which he knew almost nothing about, but she seemed to be hardly listening. When he reached to kiss her a few moments later, she was waiting and met him with an eagerness that dismayed but didn't stop him. The kiss was long, and they clung to each other. After a dozen kisses, he pushed his tongue into her mouth, and she made a small noise that sounded like a kitten purring.

His hand came up and covered her breast through the dress. She tried to break off the kiss, but he didn't let her, and slowly she relaxed again. He realized at once that she wore no bra, and his hand worked gently, around and around, searching for the hardening nipple.

When the kiss ended, she leaned away from him and looked down at his hand still holding her breast.

"Harry, I wish you wouldn't."

He smiled and rubbed her more. "Iris, do you really mean that? Deep down, doesn't it feel good, thrilling?"

Her eyes widened, and for a moment he thought she was going to cry. Then she blinked, and her smile came and she nodded.

"Darling, Harry, it does feel just wonderful, but that's what makes me frightened. I've never felt this way before."

"There's nothing to be afraid of. Iris, sweetheart, I think I'm in love with you!"

She gave a little cry of joy and pressed against him, kissing him so hard it hurt his lips. He eased their bodies apart and moved his hand, pushing it under the neckline of her dress until he held her bare breast. She made the little kitten noise again, and gently he began pushing her sideways on the couch. A minute later he lay half on top of her, his hand around her breast, his lips covering hers.

That's when he was sure. Iris McGrew would do anything he wanted her to do, right now and later on. He had won. She would protest a little, maybe cry once, but before long he would have her clothes off and would be rolling with her on the bed. He grinned. Seduction was one of the arts a man never forgets. It had been ten years since he'd slept with a woman, but he had all the old savvy.

Hector picked up her hand and moved it down to his own crotch and pressed it there. She moaned softly.

An hour later they lay naked on her bed, arms around each other, resting in delicious comfort. He rubbed her nipple until it hardened and stood tall. They both giggled.

"Darling Harry, I don't know when I've ever been so happy. I'm overwhelmed. It was so beautiful. I had no idea!"

"And it gets better and better," Hector said. He bent and kissed her breasts, and she reacted, squirming, at once panting and passionate. They made love again, more slowly, with more teasing and sex play, then they rested.

"Iris, I've been talking about my business all the time. Tell me what you do. I know you work in a bank."

"Yes, I'm in the corporate transfer accounts section. It's interesting, but the sums of money that are moved around are so huge, it doesn't really seem like money anymore."

46

She went on for ten minutes explaining what she did and how parts of the process worked.

"So when a big company needs, say, a million dollars quickly in its San Francisco office, someone simply contacts our computer and orders it to send the money out there. It's all done by computer within a few seconds with no other human contact. Sometimes we use Bankwire II, a cooperative banking computer operation, and sometimes some other operation."

"I don't understand," Hector said. "Can't one company transfer money from some other firm's account that way?"

She laughed and sat up, shaking her breasts at him.

"No, no, no. It's much more complicated than that. Each company has its own set of closely guarded code numbers. They dial the phone and get in touch with the bank's computer that handles their account. Then the computer asks them what account they are looking for, and when that is punched in, the computer says that this is a restricted account or something like that and asks for an authorization code. That is usually three or four numbers or letters. The company can set up any codes it wants to. That's part of my job, to coordinate the number codes so none of them are the same.

"And then the computer gives somebody a million dollars?"

"No. Even after the first authorization code, there usually is another password, double-checking key numbers. This would be for accounts that deal in large amounts of cash. In my section General Motors might have a secondary number and the computer would demand that double check before asking for any process. Oh, a process is simply an action the computer can take, such as withdrawing money or transferring funds."

47

"Hey, this is crazy. I never knew banks did anything like that. I should get a special account like that for my brokerage firm."

"Not unless you have an average balance of over twenty million dollars. That's the minimum for some of these accounts."

He laughed. "Well, that lets me out. But what about a big outfit like, oh, say, Bainbridge Technical. Do they work through your bank? How would they do it?"

"Matter of fact we do have Bainbridge. It's one of my biggest accounts. They change their numbers every month just to be safe."

"I'm still not sure how it works," he said. "Go through the routine for me again. I hate not understanding something like this."

He bent, kissed her, and pulled her over on top of him so her twin peaks hung straight down. He chewed on each one. She moaned and giggled and began explaining the procedure to him again.

"First, someone at the company dials a special phone number to patch into the computer."

"Well, come on, let's get on your phone and do it!"

"We can't, silly. We'd get a disconnect because that number has to be dialed through a phone that's connected to a computer terminal. There's no voice on the other end to answer it."

"What's a computer terminal? A dead machine?"

She laughed. "No, it's a little piece of electronic equipment you use to talk to the computer. You really don't know anything about computers, do you, Harry?"

"Just as much as I need to for my pocket calculator, to figure the percentage of my commissions."

They both laughed about that, and he began working one hand up her leg.

"Well, you dial in this number and then type on the

terminal printers. That's a regular typewriter keyboard that's built into this machine. You tell it what you want the computer to do. The message goes to the computer. Then the computer asks you which specific account you want and what exactly you want to do with that account. Pretty soon the computer comes back, and the printer types out a question asking for the authorization number."

She lifted her eyes. "Oh, wow! I could probably get fired for telling you this much."

"Sure, sure. I'm the type to run right out and rob a bank, right? I'll just pop my terminal out of my pocket and wire it to your phone and rob Bainbridge blind!" He laughed along with her, his hands working closer and closer to the top of her leg.

She bent and kissed him. "Oh, Harry, I can't even think when you touch me down there."

He moved his hand. She shivered. "You really want to know the rest of how it works?"

"Not really, but I need some more resting time. I couldn't even get it up for you now."

She giggled and went on. "Well, then the Bainbridge man would dial in the correct code numbers. For that particular account, the number is B-1246 and the code number for authorization is 1978. I can remember that one easily. The computer acknowledges it and asks for a second double check number, which this week is 211. I made that one up for them a month ago. I know that one because it's my birthday, February 11. Oh, when the computer gets that number, it says authorization complete and asks, 'what process?' Then the corporate person gives instructions for transferring of funds, or depositing, or whatever."

Hector Lattimer didn't need a tape recorder or a pad and pencil. He had a nearly perfect memory and

49

had the three numbers planted firmly in his mind. He could recall them whenever he needed them. He went for the bottle of champagne and filled two glasses. The drunker she was the better from now on out. He didn't want her to remember this part of the night too clearly.

They drank champagne and made love until after 4:00 A.M., and when the alarm went off at 7:00 A.M., Iris was so smashed she could hardly move. He woke and tried to get her awake. At eight he finally got her sober and awake enough to call in sick, and she went back to bed.

He left about nine and said he'd be back to nurse her hangover that night. She made him kiss her three times before he left.

Iris McGrew felt as if her head would split into a hundred pieces, but she had never been so wonderfully happy and contented in her life. How had she missed out on the marvels of sex for so long? At least now she could make up for lost time. What did they talk about between times? She had a vague, uneasy feeling that she may have spoken of some bank things that she shouldn't have, but she couldn't remember what any of it might have been. Anyway, Harry knew nothing about computers—he had told her that. And a husband and wife should confide in each other. Husband? Yes, she knew that she would try every way she knew how to marry Harry. And if that wouldn't work, she'd ask him to come live with her. Roommates, without marriage? Twenty-four hours ago she wouldn't even have considered living unmarried with a man. What an astounding difference a few hours could make!

When Hector Lattimer left her apartment, he wasted little time, walking quickly through the two inches of new snow on the sidewalks and heading back toward his own apartment about a mile away.

The snow had made a gigantic traffic snarl on the streets. There would be no chance to get a cab and no place to drive if he found one. The brisk walk worked off any semblance of the hangover he had from the night before. He did feel strangely sore and knew he had used some muscles that hadn't been tested for a long time. That would pass. The important thing was that he now had the numbers, and he was all ready to use them!

Back in his hotel room, he ordered a big breakfast, had a shower and a quick shave. By the time he finished in the bathroom, the breakfast arrived and he ate.

Hector put the tray in the hall, snapped the chain lock on his door, and opened the portable suticase computer terminal. He sat down to work.

Computer terminal plugged into wall socket? Check.

Telephone dial tone strong and steady? Check.

Phone handset put in coupler in terminal? Check.

Nervously he dialed the number that hooked him into the bank's computer and watched the terminal. There were a few seconds of silence before the typewriter hummed into action.

"SIGN ON," the terminal typed out from the computer.

"Refer Account B-1246," he typed on the terminal. It typed it out on the accordian-fold record sheet in the typewriter and sent the message to the computer deep in the bank's computer room.

At once the printout chattered back:

"ACCOUNT B-1246. RESTRICTED. REQUIRES KEY CLEARANCE."

Hector read off the number Iris had provided last night so unknowingly and typed it in.

"KEY B-1978."

"KEY B-1978. CORRECT. WHAT IS SECONDARY CHECK KEY?"

"Key 211." Hector typed with his one good hand, using the hunt-and-peck system.

The computer resonded.

"WHAT PROCESS?"

"Begin Process 616."

"BEGIN PROCESS 616. WHAT TRANSACTION? #1. TRANSFER FUNDS TO ANOTHER ACCOUNT. #2. TRANSFER FUNDS TO ANOTHER BANK. #3. FREEZE ALL FUNDS IN THIS ACCOUNT. #4. DEPOSIT FUNDS. #5. WITHDRAW FUNDS.

"Begin transaction code number 2," Hector instructed.

"WHAT AMOUNT TO BE TRANSFERRED?"

"Transfer two million U.S. dollars."

"TRANSFER TWO MILLION DOLLARS TO WHAT BANK? WHAT ACCOUNT?"

"Transfer to Hanover Savings & Trust Bank, Chicago, account #437-8418."

The computer came right back, repeating the information.

"TRANSFER TWO MILLION U.S. DOLLARS TO HANOVER SAVINGS & TRUST BANK, CHICAGO. COMPLETED."

A moment later the printout typed again.

"WHAT PROCESS?"

"Process completed," Hector typed in, feeling the beginnings of total joy filtering through his consciousness. He snapped off the terminal, and replaced the phone, and slumped in the chair.

He had just sotlen two million dollars!"

It took a few moments for him to feel the impact, to realize that the second step was over. He was a millionaire! He had only to go to the bank and pick up the money.

Hector looked down at his withered hand and began to laugh. One job Bainbridge wouldn't give him was an electrical engineering supervisory position where some light typing was involved. They said he couldn't do the job with one hand. Well, he had typed with one hand this morning, and even with the hunt-and-peck system he had just acquired two million dollars. His typing turned out to be quite good!

Hector sat there laughing at the stupidity of huge corporations and how easy they were to steal from. He laughed until tears rolled down his cheeks, tears of joy, revenge, and more than a little sadness.

Chapter 6

CASHING IN, CASHING OUT

Hector Lattimer shivered where he sat next to the computer terminal on his hotel room bed. He felt a rush of great affection for the suitcase of metal, plastic, and wiring.

Two million dollars! He had done it. After so much planning and work, it was hard to realize that part of his dream had come true.

He went to the bathroom to get cleaned up. At once he went out of the bathroom and back to the phone. He had to call the bank and tell them he would be coming in. You don't just drop in on a bank and pick up two million. Not that he was getting it all in cash, but they would need enough time to check things out.

He made a call to the Hanover Savings & Trust Bank and asked for the operations officer. Hector explained casually what he needed: $500,000 in cash that afternoon in hundreds and another $1.5 million sent to his Switzerland account so his partners there would have it for the next banking day. He suggested they use Bankwire II and the intertie with Europa Bankwire.

"Yes, Mr. Anderson, we can arrange that for you. I'll need your account number. Are you sure you want the $500,00 all in cash? We could give you five cashier's checks."

"No, Mr. Lanceway. I must have it in cash. I don't really want the cash, but it's required in my operation. I'll be at your desk at two-thirty. Will that give you enough time?"

"Yes, sir. I'll see to the matter personally and look forward to meeting you."

"Good, Mr. Lanceway. I'll see you this afternoon."

Hector hung up, smiling. Very soon, now, very soon!

He shaved with his left hand, using the electric razor, and combed his sparse hair precisely. He thought about his planning. It had taken him six months to negotiate opening a numbered Swiss bank account. Such an account could not be traced back to its owner, since Swiss bankers are extremely jealous of the privacy of their account owners. Not even Swiss police may learn the identities of such account owners unless they can prove massive fraud or illegal operations.

Hector wore his deep blue, three-piece suit and looked like a successful businessman. He put on a thick, false moustache and the nonprescription glasses that were stylish, expensive, and had a medium tint to help camouflage him even more. He wore gloves to hide his withered right hand and would sign his name as he had done for three years now using his left hand with the glove on.

That afternoon the meeting with Mr. Lanceway was quick. He said hello to the man and identified himself. Mr. Lanceway swallowed once slowly, then rose and said Mr. Anderson would complete the operation with Mr. Zumwalt, the vice president in charge of corporate accounts. He was ushered into a closed office and a smiling bear-sized man with a booming voice.

"Ah, Mr. Anderson, I haven't had the pleasure of meeting you before. I'm Milt Zumwalt in corporate accounts. We have everything set up the way you requested. All we need is your check to cover the amount for our machines. Then we can get things underway."

"Yes, I understand. Thank you, Mr. Zumwalt. You have a most efficient operation here. I approve of that. I may bring over some of my other accounts."

Zumwalt beamed.

Hector wrote out the check with a flourish as he had practiced with the Anderson name and handed the paper to Zumwalt. The banker studied the signature a moment, compared it with a signature card he had on his desk, and smiled.

He lifted a small attache case from the side of his desk and opend it. "I think you'll find the $500,00 is all here, Mr. Anderson. We've used the prewrapped bills for convenience. As you see, there are fifty one-hundred-dollar notes in each packet, and there are one hundred of the packets. That makes $5,000 per stack, and that times the one hundred bundles gives us the half-million dollars. Of course you're free to count each stack of bills if you wish."

Hector picked up one of the bundles of new bills and saw that they were in serial order. But the different bundles didn't seem to be consecutive. It wouldn't matter. He smiled at the banker.

"Mr. Zumwalt, I wouldn't consider a count. If you trust the federal reserve to count the hundreds correctly than I'm sure I can trust them as well." He closed the case and nodded.

"Now, about the transfer to Switzerland. You'll use the Europa Bankwire II connection?"

"Yes, Mr. Anderson. You're certainly well-informed on banking operations. Most people have never heard of Bankwire I, let alone the new Bankwire II. The Europa connection went into operation less than two months ago. Yes, we've cleared with the Bankwire computer in New Jersey, and all we have to do is punch it up in our computer room. I have your check, so I'll phone her now, if you have a moment?"

Hector inclined his head slightly, giving his approval in what he hoped was a dignified and yet casual manner.

The bank official made a call, waited a few seconds, and smiled to Hector. "Well, that's it, Mr. Anderson. The transfer has been made, and your money is safely in your Lausanne bank. You should receive some kind of normal documentation on it, depending on the banking institution you're using."

Hector smiled, shook hands with Zumwalt, and walked out with the small valise. He wasn't sure if the banker had intended for him to keep it, but it seemed little enough for the bank to do for a multimillion dollar depositor.

Once on the street Hector glanced down at the attache case. They hadn't even asked if he wanted an escort to another bank or home! He had a half-million dollars in his left hand!

He caught the first cab he could hail and told the driver to go along the lakeshore toward Belmont Harbor Park. He left the cab there and walked around a bit, then realized that anyone could rob him. He promptly got in another cab and returned to within a few blocks of his apartment. The two cab rides were designed to make it harder for anyone who tried to trace him through the cab companies. He hoped it worked. All the time he kept the case gripped tightly in his good left hand.

As he paid the cab driver and left him a three-dollar tip, he was feeling great. He still found it hard to believe. Now he was home free and clear. He had all the money out of the first bank and safe. He even had $500,000 in his hands! He was a multimillionaire! And that was without any taxes.

This was only the start. He would have ten times that much before he was through, and Bainbridge would be crying for mercy, screaming for him to stop, begging him to ease off. That was the part he would enjoy the most.

As soon as Hector opened the door to his apartment, he knew something was wrong. The air smelled strange—smoke. Then he remembered. The sickly sweet smoke of marijuana! That could mean only that Monty was back. He'd caught Monty smoking pot two months before he finally left the last time, for good. Hector had no desire to be arrested for marijuanna or anything else his crazy brother was using. Monty had been a late-life child and was just past his twenty-first birthday. Sometimes he seemed more like a son than a brother to Hector. But now that their parents were both gone. . . .

Hector closed the door and looked around the room. A youth slid out of the bathroom and leaned against the wall. He was half a head taller than Hector, his face gaunt with half-closed, running eyes. His hair was shaggy, uncombed, and the sweat shirt he wore looked as if it hadn't been off him in a month. He showed stained teeth and an expression that was both pained and angry. He was hurting. Even Hector could tell Monty needed a shot of some kind of dope.

Monty looked at the middle of the floor where a pillowcase held a stack of small items that could be easily hocked.

"Why did you come back, kid?" Hector asked.

"Why do you think? You got any money on you? Ain't this about the time your check comes?"

At one time Hector could handle Monty, even when he was wild and raving on pot or pills or even horse. Hector knew just how bad those trips could be. But now Monty was a grown man, and Hector didn't think that he would be a match in a physical struggle, even without his withered hand. As he watched, two more sleazy youths edged into the living room. Monty grinned.

"My backup, old man. You got any power?"

Hector held up his hands in futility.

"Now, I won't ask you again, old man. You got any money?"

Hector stared at the three angry faces for only a moment, then took his billfold out and removed the money inside, a little over $300 in twenties and tens.

"Here, it's all I've got. My check came last week."

"That's all? What about that big score you was gonna make with them exemployers of yours? We need a hundred a day for smack, man. How long you think this is gonna last?"

Monty charged forward, grabbed the bills from his brother's hand, and ran out the door into the hallway. His two companions yelled and ran after him.

Hector sat down heavily on the bed staring out the open door. Monty was a defeat he had admitted over a year ago when the kid got on drugs. There had been countless hours of talk, of persuasion, of interviews with Drug Rehab. Nothing worked. Monty went into harder and harder drugs.

Hector got up and closed the door, putting on the

chain lock. He wouldn't let Monty's sudden presence spoil his celebration. No. He deserved a small party of some kind. But first he had to hide the attache case that he still clutched. It was a good thing the boys hadn't looked inside.

He knew that any of the three of them would have gladly killed him just now for the half-million, or even for the rest of the $15,000 in his dresser. They hadn't found it, or they wouldn't have been looking for more.

He would spread out the $500,000 in various checking accounts so he wouldn't attract attention. All under his real name, he decided. But until then he needed some good place to put it.

At last he chose a cardboard box of old letters, records, and files from the closet. He dumped it out, put the attache case in the bottom and piled on all the letters, boxes of canceled checks, files, and magazines back in the box. No one would ever suspect anything of value in there.

Hector picked up the radio, his spare watch, the camera, and the tape recorder from the floor, and half a dozen other small items the boys thought they could hock, and put them away. Then he looked at the computer terminal. The case had been opened, but nothing was harmed. The fanfold printed paper was still in place. The kids might have read it, but they wouldn't have understood it anyway.

He sat down at the terminal, plugged it in, and checked the telephone dial tone before he slid the handset into the coupler on the terminal. Quickly now he punched up the dial with the telephone number he had used before to get the bank. The computer came on line:

"SIGN ON." the computer printed.

"Call for transaction log processing, TLP-459"

"RESTRICTED PROCESS. KEY RELEASE NEEDED."

Hector typed in the number he had been told would work.

"Key TLP-1413-2-22." It was the key and the month and the day of the action he wanted to examine.

"CLEARED. WHAT PROCESS?"

"Special maintenance procedure 733. Correct transaction for Account B-1246."

"SPECIAL MAINTENANCE PROCEDURE. WHAT TRANSACTION ON ACCOUNT B-1246?"

"Delete all mention of transfer two million U.S. dollars to Hanover Savings & Trust Bank, Chicago, to account #437-8418."

Hector sat there, hunched over his million-dollar toy, waiting for the reply. He knew it would take longer to clear the transaction from the log than it did to make it. He wasn't transferring the money back, simply erasing the transaction from the log and the computer's memory so there would be no record of it ever being made.

This was the same type of procedure that master programmers used to clear up records after some problem developed with a computer, such as during a power outage when some transactions got into one element of the computer but were not recorded on the transaction log. He wiped a line of sweat from his forehead even though the hotel room was chilly.

At last the IBM typewriter in the terminal chattered into action:

"SPECIAL MAINTENANCE PROCEDURE ON ACCOUNT B-1246. UNABLE TO DELETE ENTRY IN LOG OF ANY TRANSACTION OVER $500,000. DELETION REQUEST DENIED."

The typewriter finished the sentence, automatically

turned to the left-hand margin, rolled the paper up six spaces, and chattered again.

"WHAT PROCESS?"

"Process completed," Hector typed in, snapped off the set, and replaced the telephone. He worried about it a moment, then shrugged. So it wouldn't clear the record for him on large amounts. It was a good gamble. His tracks were still covered. Bainbridge would still have to check each account and each transaction to find out where the money had been taken. Unless they had some kind of automatic alarm on attempted deletions of over $500,000 transactions. He'd never heard of any.

Hector had to get ready for his date. He went into the bathroom. He was meeting Iris for dinner, if she were feeling well enough. And if he knew anything about this just deflowered virgin, she would want to stay at home, maybe eat a snack, and jump straight into bed. Tonight he would not even mention the bank, just to help her forget that they had talked about it last night.

The keys for confirmation should be good for the rest of the week. He could dip into the account and get more millions tomorrow. Hector took three one-hundred-dollar bills from the bundle he had hidden in one of his socks in the dresser. The men had missed the money when they searched.

Iris McGrew get ready, Hector thought, *here I come!*

Chapter 7

TOO LITTLE AND TOO LATE

The same afternoon Hector made his withdrawal from the corporation funds of Bainbridge Technical, Mark Hardin was on the thirty-second floor of Bainbridge Tower in an office with Barbara Simpson. She had given him case studies of each of the computer crimes in their firm and laid out all of the data about each.

Mark eliminated the honest mistakes and errors and pushed those cases aside. He was more concerned with the deliberate attempts to swindle the corporation. Perhaps he could find a pattern, some system. A few of the cases had been solved and the perpetrators punished. These were one-of-a-kind thefts, done when the opportunity presented itself. None were premeditated or carefully planned.

Danny Danlow. The name kept surfacing in Mark's mind, but he could find nothing to justify it or to tie Danlow into any of the computer thefts. There had to be a connection somewhere. The coincidence was too strong. Danlow having an electronic and computer store within shouting distance of the firm seemed to Mark to be an important cog somewhere in the gearing. He still couldn't mesh it together correctly.

One of the thefts had been through the corporate transfer accounts section. Here, huge sums of cash were sent from one Bainbridge subsidiary corporation to another for services, goods, loans, and sometimes to prop up a struggling firm or to help out on a cash flow problem.

Barbara looked over Mark's shoulder, and he sensed her perfume before he realized she was there. The scent was different today, like dew-sprinkled rose petals, subtle, and, he was sure, expensive.

"Corporate transfers, yes, that is a problem," Barbara said. She tightened her face into a frown, clouding soft green eyes for a moment. Then her brows lifted. "But there is absolutely no way we can phase out that system. The entire corporate structure relies on it for quick support and backing when needed. Some days those accounts have two thousand transactions involving more than a quarter of a million dollars each. We might send ten million to a subsidiary in Paris, London, or Rome. It's routine."

"And the computer does it all?"

"Practically, with instructions generated on this end and only after a series of computer double checks and code numbers."

"Sounds like a perfect setup for a dedicated software embezzler."

"It's as fail safe as we can make it from a security standpoint. Well, that's not quite true. We could make it much more complicated and insert a voiceprint clearance, but that would involve a small fortune in retrofit and reprogramming, and so far management has not considered it vital. Last year we lost $85,000 from our corporate accounts. It was done by an insider. The money was not recovered, but the embezzler was caught. To retrofit and reprogram now and equip our offices would cost more than a quarter of a million dollars."

"It might be a cheap price to pay for tighter security. What if somebody gets the keys and grabs ten, twenty, even thirty million at a crack? Then how expensive would your new security look?"

"It hasn't happened yet, and I've tightened up the use of those clearance code numbers. Authorization is now more difficult."

"Miss Simpson, have you ever heard of a man named Danlow?"

She frowned for a moment and shook her head. "No, that's not a familiar name. Should I know him?"

"I hope not. He's an expert on computer crime, and he's in the Chicago area. In fact, he has a computer store less than a mile from here."

"Is he involved with this extortion?"

"Let's hope not, Miss Simpson."

Mark looked at the stapled sheaf of papers a secretary brought to him. He'd asked for the names previously. They were persons who had been fired, retired, or laid off by the home office in the past year. He should have asked for numbers only first. There were one-hundred-seventy-nine retired, one-hundred-forty-seven fired for cause, and four-hundred-eighty-seven laid off and eligible for rehiring when work loads increased.

Barbara Simpson grinned at him. "I hope you're not going to interview all of them looking for one malcontent?"

"Not unless you want to help me. What about the coding numbers you talked about, the clearance authorization plan you worked out so neatly?"

"Only four persons in the Chicago area have the coding numbers."

"But there must be some people in your subsidiaries who have access to those numbers for transfers," Mark said.

"No, we use Bankwire II. The request comes in by the computer, and then usually there are phone calls negotiating, working out the details. When the decision is made, the local people authorize the transfer. That's the only way it can work. Besides the extortionist who phoned and was on the tape sounded local."

"How can you tell?" Mark asked. "With direct dialing he could have been in Atlanta or Dallas or Nogales or even Broken Bow."

She nodded, the frown lines showing again. "Yes, that's true."

"For starters, I want to talk to each of the persons in this building who has access to the numbers. You can stay in the room. I'll simply interview them and ask some questions."

She touched her chin with her hand and walked around the desk. "Curious. You're sounding less like an IRS man all the time."

"That's the secret of my success."

"You want those four names—we'll let the computer give them to you. In here at my desk."

They went into her office where she sat down in the high-backed swivel chair and pushed a button. A computer terminal swung into place. It had an enlarged eighteeen-by-twenty-four-inch screen for maximum display.

"I like the screen rather than a printout because it functions so much faster. Of course, you have no record."

She typed a few words on the typewriter and saw them on the screen setting up a process.

"Now, you want the four persons who are cleared to utilize the authorization codes for instigating action in the corporate transfer accounts?"

Mark nodded.

Before she could ask the computer for the names, her phone rang.

She picked it up and listened.

"Miss Simpson. This is the computer confirmation room. We have a strange one here."

"A theft?"

"We're not sure. We have a report from the bank computer on our tie-in reporting that it had had a request for an erase order through a special maintenance procedure involving transaction log processing. The item was a two-million-dollar transfer. The erasure request was denied about an hour ago. I just caught up with it but thought you should know."

"Check back on your own transaction log and see if any such authorization was made for such a transfer to that bank and to that account."

"Yes, ma'am, just a moment, please."

She looked at Mark, eyes hooded now with concern. She held onto the silent phone, turning slowly from one side to the other in a small, nervous dance.

Sound came back to the phone.

"No, Miss Simpson. There is no such input authorization for a two-million-U.S.-dollar transfer to the Hanover Trust & Savings Bank. We have no corporate accounts there at all."

"Give me that account number from corporate transfer again to double-check."

"Yes, it was B-1246 to Hanover."

"Thanks. I'll see what else the computer can tell me." She hung up and worked over the keyboard on the terminal, asking the computer questions, then connecting with the bank computer and asking it questions.

She unlocked a desk drawer and took out a small booklet, found the right page, and contacted the bank's computer again. A moment later she snapped off the terminal, turning slowly to Mark.

"Well, someone has done it. I don't know if it's the extortionist or not. He said he had the codes, the authorization numbers." She sighed and leaned back in the chair blinking rapidly. She rubbed her eyes. "I will not cry, dammit; I will not cry!"

"Then it was a two-million-dollar theft?"

"That seems to be so. The withdrawal date was today."

"Did you get the number of the account the money was transferred to?"

"Yes, Hanover Trust & Savings 437-8418, a business account."

"Phone them and ask if the money is still in the account."

"They won't tell me."

"Try them. They might."

Barbara scowled at Mark to cover her quivering chin and made the call. She explained her position in the company and talked to the operations officer.

"Under the circumstances, I'd like to know the balance on account number 437-8418."

"Oh, yes, I'm familiar with that account. It was extremely active today. The balance now is . . . $245.78."

"Was there a large deposit and withdrawal today?" Barbara asked.

"Yes, there was—two million dollars in and out, today."

When she told Mark, he said they should get right

down to the bank and see if they could get any more facts. She told the operations officer they would be right over to see him.

Twenty minutes later they got out of a cab in front of the Hanover Trust & Savings Bank and went inside. A secretary pointed them toward Mr. Lanceway's desk in the lobby-type open bank. Mr. Lanceway greeted them and nodded to the first question.

"Oh, yes, I certainly do remember Mr. Anderson. Mr. Charles Anderson, account 437-8418, who just put two million through this account. We didn't have it long, but we think we'll get more of his business soon."

"Well, I hope you don't," Barbara Simpson said flatly. "The man is a criminal, a thief, and that was stolen money you gave him. We're holding you personally and corporately responsible. Our lawyer will talk to you tomorrow."

"Oh, no, Miss Simpson, you must be mistaken. This gentleman was neat, quiet, a good man. I'm sure you are not talking about the same person I am."

"Would you describe this Charles Anderson, please?" Mark said with such a cold, deadly tone that Mr. Lanceway shivered.

"Yes, certainly. He's about average height, not fat, neat fellow, good dresser, suit, vest, gloves, even, and he spoke well. Educated is my guess. I'd say he's about thirty-five to forty and from the Chicago area somewhere from the way he sounded."

"How did he take the money?" Miss Simpson asked.

"Now that I remember precisely. He took $500,000 in cash, hundreds he asked for, and the other one-and-a-half million was sent by Bankwire II computer to Switzerland."

"Into a numbered account?" Mark asked.

"Why, as a matter of fact, it was."

"Can we have the number, please?" Mark asked.

"Oh, I'm afraid not. Confidential, I mean it's not ethical . . ."

"But his stealing two million dollars from Bainbridge Technical is ethical? I think you'd better give us the number and everything else you remember about him. Age, coloring, mannerisms. . . ."

"Certainly not!" Lanceway said sharply. "You keep saying he's a criminal. But we have no indications whatsoever that there was anything illegal about this transaction. Nothing but your unsubstantiated accusations. When you can show us that there was some law broken, then we'll be glad to cooperate with you and with the police."

"Now just a minute!" Barbara said, her green eyes flashing, furious.

Mark stood and caught her elbow. "Thank you very much, Mr. Lanceway. We'll keep you informed about the progress we're making on this case. You'll be hearing from us soon."

Mark urged the girl forward, and they walked out of the big lobby to the street. She was still so angry she couldn't talk. She sputtered and at last turned to Mark.

"I was ready to scratch his eyes out, that slippery little jerk," she said.

Mark hailed a cab and got her inside. He told the cabby to go to Bainbridge Tower and then looked down at the girl.

"That's the big problem with white-collar crime. First you have to convince someone that there has been a crime committed!"

Chapter 8

LOGICAL MATHEMATICAL PROGRESSION

The next morning, as soon as Hector Lattimer got up, he checked the radio news. Sure enough there was a story:

"A high-level spokesman for Bainbridge Technical, the giant electrochemical conglomerate based here, said early today that the rumors are true. Yesterday a slick computer expert stole two million dollars from the big firm. The spokesman, who refused to be identified, said it was almost certain that the theft was done by an inside person, since top secret data is needed for a person even to locate the right account.

"There is no insurance for the loss, and the spokesman said that prompt action would be taken to remedy the situation. In other news. . . ."

Hector turned off the radio and smiled as he made coffee. How sweet it was! He had done it, and now the whole world knew that Bainbridge had been swindled. Oh, they didn't know Hector Lattimer's name, and never would, but he had pulled it off! Today a lot of little people were laughing at Bainbridge Tech. They knew and would appreciate it.

Hector took out the cigar he had been saving, and withdrew a hundred-dollar bill from his wallet. He lit the corner of the treasury note with a match and watched it burn. Then he lit the cigar. The hundred-dollar bill kept burning. He was amazed at how slowly the money burned. At last it turned to an ash, but he could still see the picture. He had dropped the flaming bill in an ashtray. Now he smashed the ashes into rubble. That's what he wanted Bainbridge Tech to be: *rubble!*

He spent the rest of the morning buying a new suit and six new shirts. After all, he was a millionaire; he should dress like one. Besides he didn't want the bankers to remember his one blue suit in case they started comparing notes. The next step: he had to talk to Iris.

He phoned her to confirm their lunch date. She was still shaken by the news of the theft, but he assured her it had nothing to do with her.

They met at the Open Country Restaurant at 11:30 to beat the noontime jam. The eatery was only a block from Bainbridge Tower. She wore the same brown-and-white skirt and white blouse that he had discovered was her standard uniform.

When he first saw her, she had a long, sorrowful face, but his white florist's box changed that to a broad smile. He gave her a thirty-dollar corsage.

"Oh, my! I've never had an orchid before! You shouldn't have, Harry. What's the big occasion?"

"Iris, when a man loves a woman, he doesn't need a big occasion."

She gave a little cry of joy, but managed to hold back the tears as she leaned forward and kissed his cheek right there at the table. She'd never been forward like that before.

Iris took a deep breath, shaking her head slowly, "Oh, Harry, you have no idea how badly I needed that affection, that caring. It's been three months to the day since we first met." He reached over and kissed her lips, and then she did cry, smiling joyful tears.

They ordered, and the food was delicious and expensive. As they ate, Hector began probing about the bank.

"I did see the story in the paper about the money, but it took me half the morning to realize that it was your bank. I'm not very smart about these high finances."

"Oh, it was our bank all right. And worse, it was one of the accounts I work with. I have almost forty others, but this is the biggest. I hope I don't get into trouble over it."

"You? How can you? You didn't have anything to do with it. And you even came up with the superhard code words or something like that, you said. Will all that be changed now? I mean, did you have to work hard this morning, changing things?"

"Work hard?" She laughed. "I worked my nose right down to the bone, ground it down, to come up with a new plan. But I have one." She shook her head slowly. "Nobody on earth can break this one. I'm really proud of it."

"All that high finance fooling around is beyond me. I keep worrying about a quarter of a point on the stock ticker. That big banking talk gets me confused in a hurry."

"Oh, I bet you could catch on to banking easy. The system isn't that hard if you understand the keys. Here, let me test you for math aptitude. If I said two, four, six, what would the next logical number in the progression be?"

"Eight?"

"Yes, right. Now this one is harder. If I said eleven, then twenty-two, then two-hundred-twenty, then two and two tenths, and then four and four tenths, what would the next number be?"

"That one I don't understand at all. Just a guess 8-8/10."

"No, afraid not. I guess it's just the math major in me. First I doubled eleven to get twenty-two, then took ten times twenty-two to get 220; then I divided that number by one hundred for 2.2 and then doubled it for 4.4. The next sequence in the pattern is to multiply the last figure by ten."

"Logic and I were never good friends," Harry said, grinning.

"That's the kind of sequence I've worked out for the new numbering code system. I bet most people couldn't figure them out. Oh, there's more, including a time of day and day of the week sliding code."

"I would never be able to understand it."

"Oh, of course you would, Harry. You're very perceptive and quick. Let me test you. Now, don't hold back; this won't take but a few minutes."

She took a piece of folded paper from her purse and wrote down several sequences of numbers. Hector stared at them idly for a moment. He knew he had to be just a little dense, still not too stupid. But neither could he catch on too quickly. She was the star, and he had to help her remain the star.

It was well past her time to report back to work before she showed Hector the last sequence. "Now, what would the primary code be for say, 2:30 tomorrow?" she asked.

"Then for today at the same time, you change the

sliding code backward by one digit, and you have it. For Friday, you move three numbers the other way. Simple, but confusing to decipher unless you know at least two of the keys."

As she talked, he concentranted on the codes for today at 2:30 and Friday at the same time. That would be enough. He had them!

They walked back to the bank entrance, and he smiled, kissed her lips and said he'd see her that evening. Why didn't they go out for dinner?

"Call me about four and we'll decide," she said, a little breathless. The love she felt for this man shone out of her eyes.

He nodded, waved, and hurried across the street.

A half hour later Hector was back in his own apartment setting up his computer terminal. He was glad that his brother hadn't come back. The money must have been enough to keep them all high for two days. At least he hoped so. He had five hundred dollars hidden poorly, where they could find it if they hunted. Hector would just as soon that his brother and his dopers found the money and left him alone. That would also stop them from looking any further and maybe stumbling over the half million. He knew he should put the cash in the bank, but he liked to have it there, where he could look at it. Maybe tomorrow.

Hector took out six bank checkbooks, looked them over, and selected a bank across town this time, Lake National and put the checkbook near the terminal.

At 2:35 he plugged in the computer, checked the dial tone on the telephone, put the handset in the coupler, and snapped on the power. He used the same Bainbridge account number he had before and soon had the computer working for him. When the computer asked for the new identification and clearance authorizations, Hector gave them the codes promptly. In less than a minute from the terminal turn on, the entire process was complete.

He had stolen another two million dollars!

This time it went into the Lake National Bank under another of his aliases. There would be no need to move the money quickly this time, because he did not try to order an erasure on the transaction log. The afternoon newspaper said that was how the first theft was discovered. Without such a signpost to work from, the Bainbridge people would have no way of knowing this transaction was a fake until they checked their bookkeeping records, and that might take weeks, even months.

Tomorrow he would go down to the Lake National Bank and have all but ten thoousand of the two million sent to his numbered Swiss account.

Hector turned off the equipment and closed the suitcase, went to his refrigerator, and took out a bottle of champagne. He popped the cork and poured the bubbly fluid into a special glass he had purchased last week for this occasion.

"To my third and fourth million dollars!" he said toasting himself. "Bainbridge, you old wreck! I told you in that letter that I'd get even. I told you, and you never believed me. You just wait, you stupid old man. I'm coming after your hide!"

The hotel room door opened, and Monty slouched in. He was alone. There was none of the desperate air about him now. He wore a new shirt, had endured a haircut, had a shave, and looked almost decent.

"I need more money," Monty said.

"You always were one to beat around the bush, brother of mine," Hector said. "Nice of you to stop by and say hello. What the hell happened to the three hundred dollars?"

"That was yesterday. I had to pop for my buddies; I owed them. But then I cut out and left them. I got to thinking about what I read on the paper in that big suitcase. Ain't that some kind of a computer?"

Hector felt a chill as he realized his brother smelled a big score.

"It's only a terminal. I use it to practice giving a computer orders, only I don't have a computer. I have one game I play where I tell some big company to give me a million dollars, or two or three. I'm trying to get back into the computer field, but a lot had happened in the ten years I was out of it."

"Yeah. A game, huh? Where you get the three-hundred-dollars?"

"I told you that yesterday, my check from the company."

Monty's eyes seemed to lose interest. He looked around the room, paused at the terminal suitcase, and went on. "You got any bread left? I'm in need of a good jolt."

"You're always in need, Monty. I gave you most of the money from my check yesterday."

"I think you got more cash, lots of cash. You didn't fight enough. And you ain't been crying to me about that Bainbridge outfit. Don't sound right. They pay off big?" Monty took out a knife with a four-inch blade and began cleaning his fingernails.

"Monty, you know Bainbridge won't pay me anything more than they are, six hundred a month, retirement. Just enough to starve on. Why don't you get a job, earn your way for a change?"

The knife came up, its point aimed at Hector.

"Same old crap from you, old man. Shut up that talk, or I'll use you for knife-throwing practice."

"Monty, I can give you fifty. Then you get out of town. Go to Florida for the winter. Hitchhike down."

77

"I got connections here. I don't know no suppliers down there."

"Find them." Hector took out his billfold, and Monty moved quickly, the point of his knife touching Hector's wrist.

"Easy, old man. Easy. One bad move, and I ruin your other hand." Monty took the wallet, pulled out the bills, and gave back the leather. "Hey, that's over five hundred."

"I got some insurance money."

"Next time you tell me out front." He turned the knife and lifted it to Hector's cheek, where he raked the blunt tip down, making a two-inch scratch. "Remember that, old man. Next time tell me up front." Monty laughed, slid over to the door and left.

Hector locked the door behind him and put the chain in the slot. He was shaking so much that he almost fell down on his way to sit on the edge of the bed.

Chapter 9

COMPUTING A BIG BANG!

Mark Hardin walked into the Johnson Street branch of the First City Bank and talked with a secretary at the information desk. She took him to the man in charge of operations and personnel.

The nameplate on the desk announced the man's name was Wilbur Alghren.

"Mr. Alghren, my name is Frost. I think this letter will explain my purpose here." Mark handed Alghren a letter Barbara Simpson had prepared. It said H. Elrod Frost was a representative of the Bainbridge Technical Corporation and was empowered to talk to all persons in the bank who had knowledge of or control over the special authorization numbers used in the theft of two million dollars from the Bainbridge account.

The bank man lifted his brows. "We expected someone from your firm to come by. Terrible, just tragic! We have no idea how it could have been done. Of course, we bear no responsibility for the loss, as per our written agreements, but we did launch our own investigation as soon as we learned of the loss." Alghren was starting to sweat. He touched his forehead with a handerchief. His neat blue suit seemed to develop a wrinkle. He adjusted his glasses and tried a weak smile. "What can I do for you?"

"I'd like the names of all those individuals who had knowledge of the exact authorization numbers used. How many would that be?"

"Four. Only four. I have a sheet prepared on each of them with their work records here, social/family background, habits, everything applicable from their personnel files. This is all highly confidential information, you realize. I've been over the files; I've talked with all the people involved; and, frankly, I'm at a total loss. None of our people can have possibly been involved."

"Let's hope not, Mr. Alghren," Mark said, scanning the list. There was a vice president in charge of operations, his executive secretary, a senior computer programmer, and the head account monitor on the corporate transfer accounts.

"Is there an office I can use for the interviews?" Mark asked.

Five minutes later he sat behind a desk with a pad and pen ready for the first person. He had asked for Lester Eldridge, the vice president. Now the man sat in the guest chair at the near corner of the desk. The vice president was irritated at being subjected to another interrogation. Mark had shaken hands with the man and told him to sit down and then as the VP adjusted himself, Mark simply stared at him. The Penetrator's eyes were liquid ice, so frigid and accusing that the bank officer squirmed in his chair. He was more used to giving that stare than receiving it.

Mark eased his gaze away from the man and read from the form.

"Now, you're vice president in charge of operations, Mr. Eldridge. That's the fourth or fifth man from the top?"

"In this bank it's fourth in line, yes. I've been with this firm for twenty-seven years."

"I see that by your record. And you did know the corporate authorization numbers, or you had them in your office safe?"

"That's right. I have all the code words and numbers under my control for the entire computer wire operation. It's one of the liabilities of the job. This is the first sizable loss we've ever suffered. We hope that you can find the leak and help us stop it quickly. We realize that we are not responsible for the loss, but even so, it's tremendously bad public relations for our bank and for our corporate section." Eldridge was using his executive intensity now, which told Mark little.

Mark went through a quick checklist with the man, asking about his marriage, his personnal life. An in depth background check by a private investigation agency two months before, run routinely on all officers and persons in sensitive personnel positions, had shown no problems. Eldridge had no mistress, no other woman, no bad debts, no involvement with underworld figures. He received a salary of $85,000 plus bonuses, and his wife was back bay Boston old money. She was worth over a million dollars in her own right. He looked clean.

After ten minutes, Mark nodded, releasing Mr. Eldridge, who left the office feeling as if he had been drawn slowly through a fine mesh screen.

June Dempsy came in next. She was thirty-three, according to her file, married with one child and a husband, who was a union musician. He earned about $30,000 a year. She had been cleared by the background check previously as well. The only note was that her "gambling" notation had referred to church bingo where she regularly lost from eight to ten dollars weekly. She considered it a donation. June had been with the firm for twelve years.

"Mrs. Dempsy, I'm looking into the computer theft, as you probably know. Is it true that you have access to the authorization numbers for the corporate accounts?"

"Yes."

"Did you give any of those numbers to anyone not authorized?"

"No, I did not. And it's about time somebody came right out and asked me, instead of insinuating all the time. Of course I didn't give out the codes or keys. I'd have a hard time getting them even if I wanted to, because ninety percent of the time they're locked in Mr. Eldridge's safe, and I don't have the combination."

Mark had listened to a lot of people lie and watched their faces and hands as they did it. This woman was telling the truth. He thanked her quickly and moved to the next name.

Cloris Smith was twenty-six and black. She was divorced, mother of two, received no alimony or child support, and she was belligerent.

"What is this? A police state? You some kind of king cop or something? How come you drag me up here to answer some questions? I got work to do downstairs. I can't be running all around. What you want, man?"

Mark grinned. "We're going to get along just fine, Cloris Smith. You're not afraid to speak your mind. So what do you know about our two-million-dollar rip-off?"

"Not much. Wasn't me. I didn't snitch to nobody. Damn, if I'd even thought about it, I'd been caught first thing. I punch up the changes in the programs to take care of the new numbers and codes on the black boxes that Iris gives me. But I don't write none of them down to keep, y'know? Just like a teller and all that money they play with all day. Don't seem like real money after a time. Land sakes, but I sure hope you find that nogooder. They trying to make me look bad. Asking me all sorts of questions. Hey! I'm lucky to have this good job. No way I'm gonna mess up and lose it. I mean no way!"

Mark knew she had nothing to do with the money grab. He stood and so did she.

"Oh, that second code number for the Bainbridge corporate transfer account was 272, wasn't it?"

"Nope, it was 211 before we changed it."

Mark stared at her. She looked away, then looked back. She shrugged.

"How come you remember the second code number, Cloris?"

"Because I just made the changes this morning. Land sakes, anything that got all the excitement that account did don't take no mind to remember."

"Thank you, Cloris. You can go back to work now."

When Cloris left, Mr. Alghren came in.

"Frost, I'm terribly sorry, but we've had to change plans a little on you. This Bainbridge deal has touched off a minor panic among some of our customers, and we have had thirty requests this morning to change clearance and final authorization codings. Iris McGrew is our supervisor in charge of those operations, and right now she is swamped with work. These are accounts we can't ignore or put off. Could I ask you to come back in the morning to talk to Miss McGrew? I'm sure she'll be able to take some time then."

"I'll only need five more minutes."

83

"Sorry. I made that appeal for you myself to my superior and then went all the way to the corporate vice president and general manager, but he said to leave Iris alone today. We'll arrange for you to talk to her at eight in the morning if that would fit in with your other plans."

Mark conceded. It would give him some time to try to run down one slim lead on Danny Danlow. It was a long shot, but he had to see if Danny fit into this scheme or not. He was still betting that Danny had his nose in it somewhere.

A little after four that same afternoon, Hector Lattimer dialed Barbara Simpson's restricted office number on the thirty-second floor of the Bainbridge Tower. She picked up the phone on the third ring.

"Yes?"

"Miss Simpson, I'm disappointed in you. You haven't sent any money to my bank. You know who this is. I told you ten million, but now the fee is doubled to twenty million."

She had clicked on the tape recorder automatically as she did now with every phone call. Still her eyes widened, and her heart beat faster just to hear the raspy voice of the extortionist. She could feel his hatred over the wire. She calmed herself instantly.

"Management has absolutely refused to be blackmailed, whoever you are. You're wasting your time."

"I didn't waste my time yesterday. Remember that two million you lost via computer? The final key code word I used yesterday was 211, right? And I'll get much more unless you meet my demand for the twenty million in one chunk. It will make it easier for everyone."

"I made it clear—we don't deal with extortionists!"

"You tell Jethro Bainbridge that he'll be sorry. One of his plants in Illinois will suffer tremendous damage soon. You can count on that." He hung up, aware that he had talked dangerously long. But if the call were traced, they would find only an outdoor phone booth with an icy crust of snow on it.

He left the booth quickly and walked two blocks through the snow-free sidewalks, ignoring the bundled-up pedestrians. Hector found another phone booth on a corner and slid into it and called a remembered number. A moment later he had the man he wanted.

"Hey, Danny, I owe you some money."

"Yeah. How much?"

"This is Hector."

"Yeah, yeah, I know your voice. How much?"

"Fifteen hundred."

"You mean two hundred thousand. I know you pulled that Bainbridge shuffle."

Hector laughed. "Yeah, sure I did. If I'd scraped up two million, I wouldn't need you. I'd be in Las Vegas or on the French Riviera, living it up. What can I do with a lousy fifteen thousand?"

"Pay me, that's what. You lined up some other accounts to jump?"

"Sure, Danny, but it takes time."

"Yeah, sure. You have the cash here tomorrow, and you owe me another five hundred rent on the suitcase."

"Rent? You said I was buying it."

"So I changed my mind. Now get lost." He hung up.

A half hour later in his apartment, Lattimer went over the final plans for his night's work. He had checked the phone number two days before with the plant terminal, and it still functioned the same.

The target was the Bainbridge Tri-State Chemical plant located in River Oaks just east of the Chicago city line. It was a fourteen dollar cab fare one way.

He had checked out every phase of the operation, even the taxi ride.

Hector left his hotel slightly before 6:00 P.M. It felt like snow again, cold and blustery. He caught a cab, his heavy computer terminal and notebook safely inside the suitcase.

Less than an hour later he left the cab two blocks from the Mid-Continent Motel in River Oaks. He had selected this one carefully because it had a perfect rear view of the Bainbridge Tri-State Chemical plant.

He signed in and went to his room. After he made sure the door was locked and the chain in place, he checked the phone. Yes, it was a straight outside line. Then he went over his plan again on paper. He would dial a number from his notebook. That would put him in direct contact with Tri-State Chemical's in-plant computer. The plant had been almost totally computerized three years ago when he had worked there. He was involved in the computerization and knew everything about the system. By the time they were completed there, it was a major automation triumph. The chemical mixing was handled almost entirely by machine input and all directed by computers.

Hector plugged in the terminal and checked the dial tone. All was in order. He dialed. It worked, and a moment later the words appeared on his terminal printout.

"SIGN ON," the computer said.

Hector typed in the identification key that he had used so many times before when he worked at the plant.

"WHAT PROCESS?"

"New instructions for next mix," he typed, then fed into the terminal the chemicals he wanted mixed together and the sequence. When he had the last chemical added, the terminal was silent a few seconds, then typed back to him:

"WHAT PROCESS?"

Hector turned off the machine, unplugged it, and put the phone back on the hook. He opened the blinds on the motel window and stared a quarter of a mile across the field at the chemical plant. He wasn't sure how high it would blow, but there would be an explosion of considerable force when that last chemical was added to the other mix. It was a chemical bomb. How big the whole thing blew depended on the quantity of certain other chemicals in the immediate mix area and in the storage tanks and bins. If there were sympathetic or chain-reaction explosions, it could be huge. He checked his watch. There could be a ten-or-twelve minute batching procedure working when he countermanded the computer's mix run. He would have to wait.

As he waited, Hector made sure he was ready to leave. He had everything put away in the terminal suitcase, including the printouts. He was keeping them for his own record. Years from now he'd read back over those simple computer instructions and remember how glorious it felt and how exciting it all had been as he brought the great Bainbridge Technical Corporation to its knees, begging for mercy!

He rubbed his withered hand. It was hurting again. Even though there were no nerves in the hand to signal pain, the hand hurt. The doctors told him it might happen. Just the way an amputated leg often hurt, when it wasn't even there.

Glass—the window could blow. He moved to the doorway, standing behind the strong panel for protection. The glass would blow inward, he thought, or would it burst outward? He wasn't sure.

As he considered it, he saw a flash through the window behind him. He pushed against the door and waited for the sound and the shock wave. Moments later a roaring, growling, crackling series of explosions assaulted his eardrums. Hector knew it was more than the first simple trigger explosion. It was like a whole row of bombs going off. The first shock wave hit the motel window, bulged it inward half an inch, and shattered into the motel room, ripping and slashing the bed and the opposite wall.

Outside the motel glass flew everywhere. When the noise slackened, Hector edged the door open. In the motel parking lot, people were running everywhere. Some were bleeding, others screaming and crying. He looked at the plant. Black smoke poured from the structure. He saw flames licking at one smaller building. Green smoke billowed a hundred feet into the air. Far away he heard sirens; then more explosions buried them in sound. Hector took his suitcase and walked to the street.

People were staggering out of the motel rooms, many dazed, some with blood dripping off their arms and faces. One woman screamed from a doorway to come help her, her husband was bleeding to death. Nobody paid any attention to her. Hector walked past everyone and flagged down a cruising cab.

"What the hell's going on out there, mister?" the cabby asked.

"Something blew up, I believe," Hector said, "But I have to get back to the Loop area. There's an extra twenty-dollar tip in it for you." The cabby stared at the new twenty, took it, and flipped his meter.

"Cousin, you got it. We're moving!" He checked with his dispatcher, and turned on the standard band radio. News crashed from the speaker.

". . . no one seems to know what happened, but there is a huge fire burning in the suburban area of

River Oaks. Our first word is that a chemical plant has exploded and is now burning with secondary explosions keeping fire fighters away. No word about what caused the tragedy. The violent force of the explosions has shattered windows in a half-mile radius of the plant, with thousand of persons injured by flying glass. Hospitals and ambulances are reporting a flood of calls. We'll keep you posted on developments. Civil disaster people have just called us advising that there will probably be some evacuation needed in the downwind area from the plant. That plant is located at Drover Drive and Fourth Street. Downwind now from that area is southwest, where toxic fumes from the various chemicals are spreading.

"We're repeating, the explosion evidently took place in a chemical plant . . . Now we have the name, it's the Bainbridge Tri-State Cemical plant located in River Oaks. Those warnings for evacuation will come from police and sheriff patrol cars. Helicopters, we think, will also be used. All those who can treat themselves for cuts are asked to do so in order to leave room at the area hospitals for the seriously injured and critical cases. . . ."

The cabby snapped off the radio. "Damn," he said. "Hell of a world where something like that can happen. You'd think these big industrial outfits would be more careful than that. Hell, they should be made to build in safeguards at those plants. Never have felt good about that place since they had an explosion there three years ago." He turned and glanced at his passenger in the back seat. "Damn, now ain't that one hell of a mess?"

The cabby frowned as he looked back at the road. The guy in back must be jazzed up or something. He was sitting there actually smiling!

89

Chapter 10

A BLOODY CONFRONTATION

The Penetrator went to First City Bank the next morning, was let in the side door, and, just before 8:00 A.M., began interviewing Iris McGrew, the last of the four who had computer account authorization numbers.

Iris was twenty-nine, unmarried, and she looked tired this morning.

"I'm really sorry, Mr. Frost, but I had a hard day yesterday. I don't remember one like it before. The code number panic of February, I'm calling it."

"From what Mr. Alghren says, you know the authorization number of various accounts, including the one that lost the two million dollars?"

"Yes, that's right. That was the Bainbridge corporate funds transfer account. I still don't see how anyone could do that."

"I understand only four persons know those special numbers. Is that correct, Miss McGrew?"

"Yes, only four here at the bank. But the Bainbridge people know them. You'd have to talk to your own people to see how many executives and their secretaries have access to the numbers. I'm sure there are several. Miss Simpson, Barbara Simpson, is their computer expert. She would know all the individuals, I'm sure."

"Miss McGrew, you're unmarried?"

"Yes."

"Family live here?"

"Yes, both my parents."

"Any boyfriends?"

"I really don't think that's any of your business."

"You mean it's personal?"

"Exactly."

"Well, Miss McGrew, it may be personal, but it's still my business. I have here your entire confidential personnel file. I know every time you've been late, when you take days off, when you went on vacation, where you live, what your salary is, what your religion is, and I even have a copy of your initial application to work here. Your bank said anything I need to know about you, I can find out. To them it's highly important that they don't have another theft or a second February panic over authorization numbers. Don't you want us to catch this swindler?"

"Yes, surely."

"Miss McGrew, I'm trying to do my job, which right now is to catch this extortionist, this software computer thief. I've asked several other people if they have had any new friends lately. People they met in a bar, or at a party or lunch or on the street or during their working day. Anyone fairly new, say three or four months, who seems to be unusually interested in your work and how the bank functions, especially what the corporate transfer section does and how it works. If there had been someone like that, we might have a lead on the person involved in the theft. So that's why I'm asking you if there had been anyone, even casually, asking about your work or talking about the clearance numbers?"

Iris closed her eyes and rubbed her brows lightly with one hand to cover her face. Good lord, not Harry! She let the layers of love and affection peel painfully away and realized all the things she had told him about the numbers. In her joy and love and ecstasy, and with the help of that big bottle of champagne, she had told him more than enough to enable him to . . . oh, good lord, no! She had to think. She had to get out of here. But she couldn't faint; she couldn't act upset. She frowned as if thinking and glanced back to the smooth young man who was so good-looking.

"I'm trying to remember. There was a man who sat near me each day when I had lunch in the cafeteria. He was a messenger, I think, and for a while I hoped he was going to ask me out. But one day he didn't show up, and I haven't seen him since." She sighed and looked away.

"Really, Mr. Frost, I can't think of anyone else who has tried to pick me up or to be friendly for some ulterior purpose."

Mark noted that her hands wouldn't stay still in her lap. Her glance touched his only briefly and darted away. She fidgeted on the chair. All the classic signs of nervousness were there, but was it lying too? He watched her, turned on his cold stare, and waited. She squirmed now, then stood and walked to the window and back to her chair.

"Well, there was a woman once, a month ago. I met her in the women's lounge. She was the mannish type, short hair, wide shoulders, a real lesbian prototype. She wanted me to come to her apartment for dinner, but she was only after my body. I found out later she is an in-the-open lesbian. She was the first one I ever met, but she wasn't smart enough to try to trick anyone into giving out secrets."

Iris frowned. Harry was smart enough though! Oh, how she had fallen for his lovemaking, his flattery, his insistence that he loved her. What a fool she was! What a silly virgin of a fool!

She stood, picked up her purse. "That's all I can tell you. If I think of anything else, I'll get in touch. Really, I must get to work. We still have changes to make on authorization codes."

Mark waved, not thanking her, not saying a word. She went out the door.

Mark was sure she was lying about part of her story. She was the only one of the four who had sparked the least bit of suspicion. He decided it would be productive to follow her. He found out what time she got off for lunch and at the end of the day, memorized her phone number and home address, then checked out with Wilbur Alghren, and thanked him for his cooperation.

The Penetrator had heard the reports about the explosions and fire in suburban River Oaks on his TV that morning. He wanted to ask Barbara Simpson about it since it was a Bainbridge firm.

His try at tracking down any involvement by Danny Danlow yesterday had left him dry, no apparent connection yet between the excon and Bainbridge Tech.

When he phoned Barbara Simpson and told her who he was, she cried.

"That man called again," she said between sobs. "He told me he would destroy one of our plants. We talked yesterday afternoon. I didn't believe him. We had six men die in that explosion! And it's all my fault. Hundreds were injured, and they had to evacuate two square miles. I just don't know what to do."

"Just hold on. I may have a lead to our extortionist. It could turn into the break we need." He talked to Barbara until she calmed down and promised to come to the office that afternoon and tell her everything he had found out so far.

At noon Mark followed Iris as she left the bank to have lunch at a small pizza place three blocks away. She went at 11:30 A.M., slid onto a stool, had two slices of pizza, a Coke, and a small green salad. No one met her at lunch. She spoke to no one, and she passed no messages. Mark watched her walk back into the bank and scowled. Another hour wasted. The lady was strong. If she were involved, she had not blown sky high—she did not have a low panic point. Perhaps later.

He went to Bainbridge Tower and up to Barbara's office. She had toyed with a shrimp salad for lunch. She pushed it away. Mark put her to work quickly, checking all the accounts in the corporate transfer to see if any more cash had been stolen. It was a long and involved process, checking paper authorization order against the computer printout log.

By 2:30 P.M. she had found another two million-dollar theft. A transfer with absolutely no paper authorization at all, and to a local bank with which they did not deal.

She collapsed into an overstuffed chair in her office.

"Frost, I want to fight this, but I don't know how. What can I do, dammit, what can I do?"

He told her about Iris McGrew, and Barbara wanted to have her arrested at once, but Mark talked her out of it. "Let's see what happens tonight. Then maybe we can move."

Even as Barbara and the Penetrator talked, Hector

Lattimer was working his computer terminal magic again and stole two more million dollars. It was getting to be routine. He had to think about the $500,000 at home to understand that it was money he was working with. Honest-to-God paper dollars! He used his numbered account in Lausanne and transferred the two million directly to his account there. It presented no problem.

The bank would find out where the money went, but the input or the deposit code into his account was different from the code it took to get the money out of the account.

Hector poured another glass of champagne, realizing that the bottle was stale, and the bubbles simply didn't bubble. He didn't care. It was the ritual of the thing now that mattered.

As he drank the champagne, he phoned Iris at the bank, her private desk number. She sounded unsure, flustered.

"Is anything wrong?" he asked her.

"No, it's just this job; I'm so far behind. I don't know if I'm doing new keys or old ones by now. Everything has piled up, and now this damn changing numbers panic."

"Why don't I fix dinner for us tonight, at your place? I don't have a kitchen at mine. Will that be all right?"

She hesitated, then agreed. It would be a good place where she could sound him out, discover for sure if he were the thief. She would be careful, but she would learn for sure!

"Yes, Harry, that would be fine. There's some chicken in the freezer."

"No, I'm thinking of something a little fancier. I'll bring everything. Is your key hidden in the same place?"

"Yes, the emergency key."

"Fine, I'll see you there right after work. Now, don't stay late and spoil my dinner timing. I'll see you about 5:45 or so."

"I'll be there, Harry."

When they hung up, Hector had a strange feeling, a hint, an impression that Iris had changed. She didn't seem quite so pliable, quite so in love as she had been. Or was it just the overwork? He didn't know.

When Mark got back to the bank, it was fifteen minutes before quitting time. He waited near the employee entrance and saw Iris come out promptly at 5:15 P.M. She caught a bus a block down and rode for a half hour. Mark managed to get on the same bus and stepped off in a group well behind Iris when she exited. She didn't look around, didn't check to see if she were being followed. Maybe she wasn't in on the theft, or at least maybe she didn't know that she was. Or perhaps she didn't realize that she was an important element in a complicated chain.

She walked down a cold street to a small delicatessen, and Mark saw her buying a bottle of wine. A celebration? Maybe she did know more about the swindle than she had said. Or it could be that she simply liked wine with her home-cooked meals.

She walked two more blocks to a six-unit apartment building and went into the bottom left unit. Lights were already on inside, which could mean someone was already there or that she had a timer flip on the lights when it got dark as an antiburglary move. If she had any visitors, Mark would question them at once after they left her apartment.

It was still near freezing outside as Mark leaned against the building and tried to think warm. He hoped it would not be a long vigil.

Inside the apartment, Iris was surprised to find Harry watching TV. She smelled no cooking, and, for the briefest of seconds, her heart broke open just a little more. Harry must have had no intentions at all of cooking her dinner.

"Hey, hello!" Harry said, jumping up as soon as he heard the front door open. He went forward to kiss her, and she permitted his lips to brush hers.

"I didn't start dinner yet, because I didn't want anything to distract us when you came home." He kissed her again, more demanding this time. Then his hand closed around her breast, and she gave a little cry. His hips pushed against hers, and she felt his hardness there, pressing on her stomach. Oh, God! But it would feel good! She tried to lean away, but his hand came down the front of her blouse. Then it was all confusion—her mild protests and his insistence, and clothes dropping to the floor—until Iris knew her knees wouldn't hold up a moment longer, and she sat down on the living room's soft blue carpet. He was beside her, pulling off her skirt and her panty hose. Then his hand touched her most private place, and Iris couldn't help herself—she moaned in pleasure.

Later she sat up and looked at him. Twice they had made love there on the blue carpet, and she found it hard to believe that this man had made such a fool of her—had used her.

He leaned up on an elbow and looked at her. For one brief, wild moment she wanted to pull her clothes over her nakedness; then the thought was gone.

"Did you work through your overload?" he asked. "They should bring someone in to help you on heavy days."

"Most of it is done. Almost all of it." She wouldn't

mention the codes or Bainbridge. She'd make him
give himself away.

"That theft was terrible. Have any more shown up
on the computer?"

"I don't know; that's not my job. I just try to get
the codes right and as tough as I can make them."

"These key numbers certainly are clever, Iris. What
will you do for changes next week? I mean, can you
think of something else as sharp as those?"

"I'll try."

"What about next week? You said the Bainbridge
codes were good for this week. Can you project those
for next week?"

"Yes, they're all done."

"Test me, see if I can figure them out. I like
puzzles."

"Why are you so eager to try this, Harry?"

"I'm not eager. It's just a little game."

"No, Henry, it's more than a game with you. I
called your real estate firm today. There is a company by that name, but they have never heard of
you, and you certainly don't own the firm or work
there. Also you aren't listed in the phone directory or
the R.L. Polk book. It doesn't seem anyone knows
much about any Harry Anderson. Are you sure that's
your real name?"

He stood at once and began putting on his clothes.
"Iris, I don't like people spying on me. Why did you
do that? I've been good to you. You know I love you.
Now you treat me this way. I don't understand, Iris."

"You never did tell me how you hurt your hand,
Harry. Did it happen doing something illegal?"

He put his shoes on and laced them up deliberately. "Of course, that's my real name. I'm not happy
with you, Iris. We just made love, and now you're at-
tacking me. I don't need all of these accusations, these

98

insults." He buttoned up his shirt and stared down at her. "I really dislike your whole attitude, Iris. Is something wrong? Have I done something you don't like?"

"Yes, Harry, you have. I don't like people using me." She stood, and her face was sad and a little angry. "You used me, Harry. You met me on purpose in that pizza place, and you used me. You made me think you cared about me, and you seduced me and toyed with me, but all the time you were after the clearance numbers. I told you about them, Harry. You're the only one I've mentioned them to, so it has to be you. You're the thief. You're the one who stole two million dollars from Bainbridge Technical through a computer."

Hector had flinched when she screeched at him. He knew that the soft talk was done with Iris. His look of astonishment changed slowly to a frozen smile.

"You're quite wrong, Iris. I didn't steal two million from Bainbridge Technical. Actually I stole six million. Four million they don't even know about yet. And I owe it all to you, Iris. It took me a month just to figure out how to meet you. Then your pizza lunch paved the way. Then gradually you shared your little secret with me. So, you're just as guilty as I am, Iris. You'll spend at least twenty years in prison. Banks don't like their people to give out information like that. And don't expect me to take you away . . . even though we could live like royalty."

Iris took a quick step backward and picked up her skirt. He jumped forward and tore it from her hands. Anger, then sudden fright, swept over her features.

"No? So you don't want to go away with me? Then we'll stay here in this apartment, and you'll supply me with the codes for next week while we steal another ten million. Then I'll have enough."

She bolted for the door, but he caught her halfway there, his withered hand hooked around her neck, pulling her backward.

"Now, Iris, mustn't try to run away. That wouldn't be nice, especially since you have a houseguest." She ran toward the window, but he grabbed her arm and spun her around.

Iris screamed.

The television sound drowned out her cry. He let go of her arm and slapped her as hard as he could. She staggered backward and fell to her hands and knees. He had to silence her quickly. But he had no weapon, no club, no heavy ash tray. She looked up at him, panic giving way to pleading eyes. She realized how she had misjudged him, how she had not guessed him capable of violence. She crawled toward the door.

This was when Hector remembered the south side of Chicago, years ago, where he had seen a man kicked to death. Hector moved between Iris and the door. He gauged the distance; then his leather-soled shoe lashed out, the heavy toe catching Iris on the side of the jaw, splintering the bone upward into her mouth. She cried softly and stared at him for a second as she fell to the carpet, where she passed out from shock.

It was as if he had planned this part, too, but he hadn't. He knew exactly what to do. He had misjudged Iris. He thought she was an innocent and would remain so. He didn't expect her to catch on about how he had milked her dry about the numbers.

Iris moaned and rolled onto her back, one hand flopping near him. It would have to be a ritualistic affair—like the Manson family he had read about—lots of blood.

He ran to the kitchen and brought back six steak

knives and a sharp, serrated butcher knife. The blade bit into her wrist surprisingly easily, and the red blood flowed in a stream onto the blue carpet. He used a tissue as a brush and with her blood drew a pentragram on the wall—a five-pointed star in a circle. He made some half-remembered, half-created signs and symbols inside the circle.

Iris was groaning now, and the sound startled him. He tied her feet together with her blouse. She could have ruined it all. It was her fault if she died. She had threatened him. No one could threaten Hector Lattimer. Why had she guessed? He felt his anger rising, and the fury blinded him for a moment. He grabbed the butcher knife and began slashing her white skin, making it erupt with red streaks of blood. He cut her again and again, not deeply, but with lots of blood. She groaned and cried out.

He jumped back, saw what he had done, and frowned. Then he spotted the steak knives. He took one and plunged it into her heart. The five other knives followed, past ribs, around her breast, until all were imbedded in her chest.

He listened but could hear nothing from her. She had stopped breathing. He jumped back again.

Blood flecked his pants and shirt. He would destroy them. Using a handkerchief, he wiped everything he had touched to remove all his fingerprints. When he was sure he had it all clean, he went to the front door and started to reach for the handle. Then he shook his head.

It was too early. Someone might see him come out. The back way. There must be a back door to the garage area. There was, out the far end of the kitchen, where the door opened into the garage and storage area. She had no car. He moved silently through the dark areas to the far end of the alley. No one had seen him. No one.

His overcoat covered up most of the blood. He ran for two blocks, found a bus stop, and saw a downtown car coming. Furiously he waved it down and climbed on board, paid his fare, and went to the back of the seats. He was away free. He had done it. The only person who could give him away was silenced.

At the front of the apartment house, Mark Hardin watched the lower right unit with increasing worry. He had seen no change in the lighting, heard nothing, but still he wondered. It had been less than two hours. No one had visited her. It must have been before. She had met someone inside.

He jumped up and ran to the apartment door, working out his stiffness from the cold as he moved. He knocked. No one answered.

Mark tried the door and found it unlocked. He knocked. He knocked again, waited, and edged the door open. He stepped inside quickly and closed the panel. Two steps into the living room and he took in the death scene at a glance. He was certain the woman was Iris McGrew and that she was dead. No one was in the room—he could do nothing there. He walked out of the apartment, wiped the door handle clean and moved to the sidewalk. Two blocks down he found a phone booth and called the police about a disturbance at Iris's address. He thought about the satanic symbols on the wall and the pentagram. Authentic or not, the press would have a field day with this one.

But he had missed the killer. He had seen the girl go into the apartment alive and never come out. The killer must have been inside waiting for her, with or without her knowledge. That's what he was angry about: he had missed the extortionist and the killer. He was sure now that the leak in security on the authorization numbers was stopped. But he still had to find the killer—and soon.

Chapter 11

COLD STAKEOUT

Mark stared at the morning paper's account of Iris McGrew's murder as he waited for the phone to be answered on the other end. He couldn't forget the girl's death. He had been so close. If he'd known, he could have prevented the murder and nailed the extortioner all in one grab.

"Hello?"

"Barbara, this is Frost. I saw the paper."

Her voice held an edge, as if it were carefully controlled so she wouldn't slip over the edge into tears.

"Frost, you better get up here, I have something new to show you. I don't see how we can ignore this one."

In the cab to the Bainbridge Tower, Mark realized again the impact of what was happening. This young woman was running a multibillion dollar conglomerate, evidently by herself. She was the last and final authority. How could she do it? If it weren't true, she would not have the pressure of dealing with a massive problem such as this extortion. Where was old

Jethro Bainbridge himself? Were the rumors right? Had he died two years ago? How was this girl running a conglomerate when it usually takes a battery of vice presidents and corporate managers to do it?

Mark was going to find out.

In her thirty-second floor office, Barbara Simpson paced the thick rug, hands clasped behind her back. As soon as Mark came in, she handed him the accordion-folded computer printout. It hadn't even been torn into pages.

"Read this," she said as her greeting. Her lips were set and hard, her eyes cold. She was in walking shock and didn't know it.

Mark took the computer printout paper and read.
BARBARA SIMPSON. . . .BAINBRIDGE TOWER.
MESSAGE PROCESS:
MISS SIMPSON: YOU HAVE NOT RESPONDED TO MY URGENT DEMAND FOR FUNDING. NO FURTHER CONTACT WILL BE MADE WITH YOU. MUST INSIST THAT FUNDING NOW BE EXPANDED TO TWENTY MILLION, THIS DATE. SEND FUNDS TO ALREADY KNOWN BANK NUMBER OVER EUROPA BANKWIRE II.

COMPUTER TRANSFER VIA BANKWIRE II TO BE COMPLETED WITHIN EIGHT HOURS. IF FUNDS NOT TRANSFERRED THE BAINBRIDGE TOWER BUILDING WILL BE SHATTERED. FOR REFERENCE, CONSIDER THE TRI-STATE CHEMICAL INSTALLATION.

NO FURTHER COMMUNICATION. MUST INSIST ON THE TWENTY MILLION ON TIME OR UNTOLD DEATH, DESTRUCTION, MISERY AND TERROR WILL STRIKE BAINBRIDGE TECHNICAL. REMEMBER TRI-STATE CHEMI-

CAL. TIME NOW IS 0630, OR 6:30 A.M. CENTRAL STANDARD TIME. EIGHT HOURS ONLY!

NO SIGNATURE:

WHAT PROCESS?

Mark looked up from the coldly frightening, computer-typed sheets. He had forgotten all about Bainbridge. The man who was threatening the people here was insane, whoever he was, and with a gigantic hatred for Bainbridge Technical. Why couldn't they get a handle on him somehow? Eight hours. It was 9:30 already. That left five hours. The Penetrator thought it through again. The man wanted the money more than death and destruction. This was Mark's evaluation of the printout. So the five-hour deadline would not be for the Tower. Perhaps another building, another example?

Barbara watched him, her green eyes now clearer, not so cold, warming, but only with an effort. She was still in a mild form of mental shock.

"Well, is he serious? Can he do what he says he will do? How do you destroy a skyscraper high-rise like this that covers a whole city block?"

"He's serious, and he must believe he can do what he threatens. But his deadline is unrealistic. I think he has something else in mind first. It would take an atomic bomb to wreck this Tower. Outside of that he could hurt the building but probably not destroy it. Oh, yes, he's serious, so we have to stop him."

"Stop him? We don't even know who he is!" Her voice rose, and at once she lowered her head, touched her brow, and apologized. "I didn't mean to shout at you, it's just that. . ."

"I know," Mark said, touching her shoulder. "I've

been there. Did the police say anything more about the death of the bank employee, Iris?"

"You met her yesterday, didn't you? I've talked to her dozens of times on the phone. She seemed quiet, efficient. The radio said police are sure now that the killing was not a satanic, ritualistic affair. That was evidently a try at a cover-up."

"Now I'm sure the extortionist is also the killer and the man who stole the money by computer. It all ties together. Iris must have suspected someone and confronted him. At least we have one man and not two. This is his first big mistake, and it may help us trap him."

"How?"

"If the police come up with any good clues, they'll point to the killer and also to our extortionist. Now, let me try something else." He took a typed copy of the extortion printout and caught a cab to Iris's neighborhood. The weather was milder now but still in the low forties. Iris's apartment building was quiet; only a police hasp and padlock on her front door indicated anything was different. The rear door was fitted with the same device.

Mark settled down in his new overcoat and gloves, adjusted his stocking cap low over his ears, and walked slowly along on the far side of the street. There was no convenient coffee shop here to use for a stakeout position. At last he decided the side windows on ground level would be the best target, so he went to the alley where he could see the back door of the apartment and the two windows. Mark sat down against the steps of an adjoining house and pretended to be sleeping.

It was just after midday when Mark saw them come. A man in his twenties with uncombed hair, dirty pants, and an oily army fatigue jacket. He looked cold. The girl with him wore a man's overcoat that was too big for her. She had on a felt hat, long blonde hair cascading out of it. The hair was stringy and dirty. She stayed at the mouth of the alley as the man came in cautiously. He watched Mark for several seconds, discounted him, and went up to the rear of Iris's apartment. When he saw the police padlock, he began backing up, but before he stopped, he bumped into Mark, who caught him in a bear hug and lifted him off the ground. The girl had run when she saw Mark head into the garage.

"What's your hurry, man? We're going to have a little talk."

"I ain't done nothing!"

"You're a user."

"Prove it!"

"I don't have to prove anything, Ace. It's just you and me, and I'm bigger and meaner than you are."

"Cops stink!"

Mark tightened his grip until the kid yelped. "You're not smart at all, are you, Ace?"

"I'm not Ace. I'm Monty."

"Why were you looking at this apartment, Monty?"

"I wasn't."

"You were. Now give." Mark let go of the slightly built youth, spun around, and pinned him against the inside garage wall.

"Why, Monty?"

"Just a hunch. Nothing more."

"Thought there were goods here? She was a dealer?"

"No, thought my brother might be here. He left her address on his table one day, so I copied it down. Never know where my brother is going to land next."

"And he was giving you money for your monkey?"

"Huh? Oh, yeah, monkey. Hundred a day."

"Big animal. So who did he come here to see?"

"I don't know."

"Let's take a trip back to your brother's pad. You know where it is?"

The kid nodded.

A half hour later the taxi let them off in front of a half-respectable residence hotel. They climbed to the fourth floor, and Monty opened the door with a credit card. Inside it was a typical one-room accommodation. Clothes hung from chair and bed; remains of a quick take-out dinner on the dresser; a half-filled milk carton sat on the cold window ledge.

"Kid, sit down on the bed and don't move. Don't even breathe, Monty, or I'll break your arm."

Monty sat and waited.

Mark went through the room quickly, found the stash of five-hundred-dollar bills, and slid them into his pocket. He could check the serial numbers with that first bank. Behind the bed he found a used suitcase. It would be empty, he knew, but from long experience, he picked it up. It was heavy. He swung it on the bed and flipped it open. Mark raised his brows in surprise.

A typewriter of some sort, built-in, some black electronic boxes, and a hole just the shape and size to fit a telephone handset. He tried the phone in the hole, and it slid in perfectly.

A computer? No, too small. Maybe a terminal, a computer input terminal! He saw the accordion-folded paper along one side. It was similar to what he had read a few hours ago, only smaller. Some of it had typing on it. Gently he lifted it out and began reading.

Computer talk. Instructions to a computer to withdraw money from one account and transfer it to . . . jackpot! This was the terminal used to steal the millions from Bainbridge Technical. It was all spelled out in detail, just how it was done.

"What's your brother's name, Monty?"

The kid on the bed jumped. "Oh, Hector. Hector Lattimer. He's about thirty-five or so, got a bad right hand. All withered up. He got it mixed up with a big jolt of electricity few years back."

"Did he work for Bainbridge Technical?"

"Hey, yeah. How'd you know that?"

"Just a hunch. Think your brother will come back here?"

"Nope, not him. His shaving gear is gone and his money. He ain't showed. I've been here since last night. Nope, I think he's gone."

Mark grabbed the phone and dialed Barbara. He explained they had a break and asked her to send two plainclothes company guards to Hector's address to stake it out from the inside—around the clock. She said they would be here in half hour.

While he waited, Mark took the room apart. He found nothing. From what the first bank said Hector had withdrawn a half million in cash. Where was it? Was he carrying it around in a suitcase with him? He must have panicked and run last night after the killing. No, he used the terminal sometime this morning. Early. Monty could have been sleeping or on a trip and never known his brother was there.

The guards arrived, and Mark explained the job: to hold the hotel room and nab anyone who tried to come inside. If it were Hector Lattimer, he'd have a withered right hand. They nodded, settled down with two bags of groceries and two decks of playing cards.

Mark roused Monty down the stairs to the street.

"Get lost, punk," Mark said. "Get out of the way. You louse up this grab, and I'll hunt you down and pull your eyeballs out until they won't snap back in

110

place anymore." Mark threatened the young man with a left jab, and Monty ran down the street, screeching insults.

Mark looked for a cab. Now he knew who the extortionist was. All Mark had to do was find him before he blew up something after the eight-hour warning. It could be Bainbridge Tower, and if so, it could kill thousands of innocent people.

Chapter 12

FIRE IN THE HOLE!

Hector Lattimer sat in his new hotel room a mile from the old one. This place had some class and cost him three times what the other one had, but he could afford it. He had returned to his old room after silencing Iris and packed most of his belongings quickly.

Monty had passed out on the bed, so Hector made certain that he didn't disturb his brother. Hector left the $500 on the shelf, hoping that Monty would find it and go off on a week-long drug trip and not bother him any more. Hector had packed too fast and forgot many things. It was a spur of the moment, near panic move, and he regretted it now. He should have taken more time, planned it out as he did everything else, then packed. He had taken the cash in the new attache case, but in the last minute surge he had decided he didn't need the computer terminal anymore, so he left it in the room. He knew now it was a mistake. He would have to go back after it. But last night it had been so late, and he had both hands full, and it seemed too heavy to carry. He would have to be sure to get it. The printouts! They were all in the case. He needed them for his records on the three two-million-dollar outfoxings of old Jethro Bainbridge! He would use them word for word in his records, in his memoirs. A man had to plan ahead.

Now he concentrated, staring at the ceiling, working out the current operation. He had located the building, another small firm that Bainbridge Technical owned, near Elgin. He had given Bainbridge the eight-hour deadline just to get their attention. If he proved to them that he could blow up a building, then they would listen to his demands. His plan worked to perfection on paper, in theory, but he was a practical engineer, and he needed to try a small, scale-test operation before he went to work blowing up Bainbridge Tower.

Hector made two phone calls, took two thousand dollars in hundreds from his case, slid the money into his coat pocket, went downstairs, and caught a taxi.

Stan Silikowski was a truck driver and handyman Hector had known from his days at Bainbridge Technical. Silikowski had worked in several capacities at Bainbridge but at last was fired for knocking down his lead man and punching out the red badge supervisor who came to intervene. Silikowski had fists for brains, a six-foot-four body and plenty of muscle. That was exactly what Hector needed tonight.

He met Silikowski on the corner of 116th and Pinout streets, and they drove to the Chicago Chemical Company two blocks away. Hector went into the office wearing his fake beard and black horn-rimmed glasses and presented them with the order and a check for $5,387. The check was a masterpiece of printing, which showed the firm as Marshal Cryogenics Laboratory, with an address, phone number, and even a computer slogan. The clerk didn't bother to verify the check, just compared the amount to the invoice, looked at the address, and asked Hector where the bottle should be delivered.

"The company sent a truck, we can load it right now if that's all right with you," Hector told the bored clerk.

A half hour later they had the six-foot-long, three-foot-thick bottle of liquid hydrogen on the truck and tied down. The bottle was surrounded by its own cryogenic shielding that would keep it at the required extremely low temperature for twelve hours. After that time, if the liquid temperature rose over the limit, venting would be required immediately.

They drove along the Northwest Tollway out of Chicago at fifty miles an hour. Hector didn't want a policeman or highway trooper even to notice the truck, let alone stop them. It was a thirty-five mile ride to Elgin, and they arrived there just before 8:00 P.M. and scouted the area. The building Hector had picked two weeks ago still looked like the best one. It was four stories high, had an elevator, and was isolated enough so there would be no interest in the plant other than the building's own guard. It was a plastics firm and the first building up in this new industrial park.

At 9:30 P.M. they drove up to the metal gate and Hector jumped out and walked to the guard box where the company night watchman spent most of his time.

"Good evening. I Dr. Heinrich Strauss with shipment of special molding equipment and heat-treated plastics I deliver personal. Then I must catch plane back to Berlin."

"Yeah, that so?" the guard asked. He was in his fifties, had just retired from the Elgin police force, and hadn't lost his cop hardness yet. "Nothing on my sheet says anything about any shipment."

"Here my invoice. Come take look at load if you wish. But must hurry so I catch plane."

"Don't say? Yeah, I'll have a look." He unlocked and came through the big metal gate, leaving it a foot ajar. When the guard went around the back of the truck, Stan Silikowski smashed a steel pipe down on the guard's head, cracking it open like a tomato under a car tire. The excop died in seconds.

"All right, stop admiring your work, Silikowski! Get him inside the fence, drive the truck to the back door of the building, and close the gate. Quickly, before someone straggles past here!"

A half hour later they were ready. Hector had worked out the technical details carefully and shopped around until he found exactly the hardware that he wanted made mostly of plastic so there would be little left to identify. The pregnant vacuum bottle rested on the ground floor next to the elevator. The open-topped and open-sided elevator car sat on the ground floor. A six-inch steel reinforced rubber hose led from the cryogenic bottle and its liquid hydrogen to the elevator shaft and the half open doors.

Critically, Hector set the timer, an all-plastic device that would close a circuit in precisely five minutes, blowing off a valve allowing the liquid hydrogen to escape out the hole into the tube where the change in pressure and temperature would at once turn the liquid into a vapor and shoot it through the tube into the elevator shaft where it would float gently upward. The lighter-than-air hydrogen gas would rise the way it had in the hydrogen-filled Hindenberg dirigible.

In twenty seconds most of the liquid hydrogen would be vaporized and into the elevator shaft and drifting into almost every part of the building. The tremendous volume of the gas once liberated and changed to vapor was plenty to fill the whole building, creating a huge bomb just waiting to go off.

At precisely twenty seconds after the first timer closed letting the gas escape, the second timer would go off. The second timer was wired to a detonator on a small charge of dynamite, which would act as the primer and trigger, setting off the volatile hydrogen gas in the building-sized bomb.

Hector put the two timers in place, nodded at Stan, who knew the speed needed, and they both ran for the truck. They drove out the gate, not bothering to close it, and stopped a half mile away where they had a good view of the plant and were still near a highway.

Hector looked at his stopwatch.

"Four minutes and forty-five seconds ... fifty ... fifty-five, six, seven, eight, nine...."

The whole sky in front of them flashed with the brilliance of a hundred lightning bolts. The building seemed to lift several feet, and parts of it jetted forward and upward against a flash of orange-white light. Hector could see the walls propelled outward and spotted in the sudden flames a pear-shaped cloud that rose; he watched as the whole four-story structure sagged and crumbled into a pile of rubble ten feet high.

The cracking roar of the single explosion hit the truck with the sound of a hundred jet planes taking off, and the shock wave rocked the twenty-foot-square side of the van.

Hector sat there watching the flames licking at the remains of the building. That should be a potent demonstration for the big shots at Bainbridge. There were no chemicals here to feed the explosions. Just a regular office building like the Tower, just a building that exploded like a nitroglycerin bomb! He motioned to Stan.

"Out here at the side, Stan, I want to show you something." Hector went to the ditch side of the country road, and when Silikowski came up to him, Hector shot Stan twice in the chest with a .45 automatic. Silikowski jolted backwards and to one side. Hector walked up close and put one final bullet through the handyman's brain.

He didn't look again at the body. Stan was dead, and the link with him was gone. It was simply another routine step to be taken. Hector got into the truck and drove. He had made sure that Stan rented a twenty-foot van truck with a simple five-speed transmission, because he knew he would need to drive it away from the site. He wanted to make sure there was no hi-low range, split transmission, involved. He wouldn't be using the rig long.

Hector drove into Elgin, parked the truck a block from the bus terminal, and caught the 10:14 for Chicago. The bus was on time and left precisely as scheduled. Hector liked promptness.

On the bus he debated whether or not to phone Barbara Simpson as soon as he got back to Chicago, but decided it should wait until morning. By then she should be well-informed on how the latest Bainbridge firm had been destroyed. His bomb in a bottle was much more efficient and powerful than he had hoped. As he rode, he calculated how many bottles of the liquid hydrogen it would take to fill the west bank elevator shafts of Bainbridge Tower. He couldn't hope to fill the huge building. Or could he? He had more planning and estimating to do.

Hector Lattimer fell into a gentle sleep just before they reached the Chicago terminal. When the rig stopped, he was up and moving, eager to get his calculator and work out the volume studies on Bainbridge Tower.

"Just wait until tomorrow," he muttered to himself and ran through the depot to find a taxi.

Chapter 13

MORE DEAD THAN ALIVE

The same evening the building exploded, Mark was in Barbara Simpson's office. They had tracked down the employment records on Hector Lattimer. His picture, fingerprints, and all the data they could find on him was sent at once to the Chicago Police Department along with information about Lattimer's involvement with Iris McGrew. A letter stated that other charges would be filed against Lattimer in the morning, covering grand theft, arson, extortion, and murder.

Mark helped lay out a security blanket for the Bainbridge Tower, and they were duplicating the most recent picture of Lattimer so each of the security force guards at the Tower would have one. Lattimer might be disguised, but they knew he would be wearing gloves to cover his withered hand. Much of the security for the big building was controlled by computer, and that worried Mark, but there was no way to change the complicated system now. They would have to monitor the whole area and try to fill in any gaps. But for how long? That was always the problem with defense; it had to be one hundred percent around the clock. But the aggressor could pick and choose his time, relax, and conserve his energy.

Just after 9:00 P.M., a report came in on Barbara's computer printout telling about the explosion of the company plant near Elgin. Barbara didn't even know the firm had any operations in that area.

"Witnesses said they saw a truck speeding away from the plant, and a few minutes later it exploded like one gigantic bomb. The whole building blew up at once, from basement to fourth floor."

Mark tried a radio but could find nothing about the explosion on the news station.

Barbara sank to the sofa, her face pale from the shock of it.

"So now he's proving to us that he really can blow up a building," Barbara said. "He's insane. It was his own mistake." She went to her phone and sent her top security team to the Elgin site to discover exactly why the building blew up. It could have been accidental, but she didn't think so. She needed to know exactly how and why the building was destroyed.

"It could have been a test," Mark said. "He's an engineer, remember. He may have wanted to try out a small-scale explosion before he went for the big prize, Bainbridge Tower."

She turned to him, ready to cry, eyes pleading.

"Frost, we must find this man; we must stop him. Do you realize how many innocent people could be killed or injured if he did set off some kind of blast in this building? Hundreds might die just from panic."

"At least now we know who he is, and we know that he's out for revenge. That's the hardest kind of a man to stop. He'll probably sacrifice himself if he needs to, if he can embarrass, hurt, or even bring down the Bainbridge corporation."

"The man is totally insane."

The phone buzzed with two shorts and a long. She frowned. That signal came only from the lobby guard downstairs.

"Yes, Barbara Simpson."

"Miss Simpson, this is the lobby guard. Sorry to bother you, but there's a man here who claims he's Roscoe Bainbridge. I've never seen Mr. Bainbridge, ma'am, except in our file pictures. This man has been drinking, and he's talking wild."

"Is he about fifty, balding in front, twenty pounds overweight, about six-one, and dressed like a dandy?"

"That's him, all right."

"It's Roscoe then. Have a guard bring him up to my office here on thirty-two. I have protection here. I just don't want Roscoe to hurt himself or get lost coming up."

"Yes, ma'am."

"Just what we need," Mark said as she put down the phone.

"Oh, this is a normal babysitting chore. Usually it only happens once a month."

They talked about Lattimer, brainstorming ways they might trap him. Mark shook his head, saying the man was too smart to fall for a meeting.

When the office door opened, they saw that Roscoe Bainbridge was indeed half drunk. His tie hung loosely, his suit looked as though it had been slept in, his shirttail was out, and his eyes were red and watery. He pointed one finger at Barbara and swore. "It's all your goddamned fault, you bitch! I know it is! I know you've got Dad all doped up somewhere, and hidden, and if he isn't dead, he'd rather be. You're running the company, and I'm out in the cold."

She ignored his outburst and asked him coolly how things were going in Michigan.

"Michigan! Ha! You fooled me again, you witch. Give me my own company to run, so I can prove myself. Sure! Hell, yes. I tried. The vice presidents nodded politely and said: 'Yes, Mr. Bainbridge,' or 'Of course, Mr. Bainbridge.' Then they went right on running the company like you told them to. They didn't pay any attention to what I said. They wouldn't even let me save some dignity and be a figurehead president."

She ignored the second outburst, smiling serenely at him. "Roscoe, what would you like if you could have anything in the whole world? I mean anything. Now the last time you said Farrah Fawcett-Majors, so you can't use her again. What would you like?"

"Anything?" he asked, responding to her immediate question but totally confused by her sweetness, her change in subject, and her lack of reaction to his anger. "Hell, I don't know."

"Let's ask the computer. I bet the computer will know exactly what you want more than anything else in the world."

She went to the desk terminal and flipped on the switch, punched up some numbers, and initiated a process. Then she typed in the question: "What would Roscoe Bainbridge want more than anything else in the world?"

It took only a fraction of a second before words flashed on the screen: "THE 12-METER RACING BOAT *COURAGEOUS*."

Roscoe read the words on the screen, then said them out loud.

"The *Courageous!*" He stood there behind Barbara with a strange little-boy smile on his lined face. "*Courageous* is the best goddamned twelve-meter sailing boat in the whole crazy world! Sixty-six feet of beauty. Twice winner of the America's Cup! A crew of ten, the wind, the sleek beauty cutting through the waves off Long Island. Sweet mother! I saw her race once off Newport. Sweet mother, but that would be a thrill. Your computer is right. I'd kill for that boat."

"Then she's yours, Roscoe. Your father arranged it yesterday. It's for your birthday."

Roscoe dropped on the sofa, and his eyes brimmed with tears. Then he gulped, backhanded the tears away, and stood, slowly, almost sober now. He smoothed down his hair, straightened his tie, and tried to pull himself into some semblance of proper form.

"Now, Miss, I must see Father to thank him for this glorious present, if for nothing else. Common courtesy demands it. I know where he is. Yes, I have spies too. A few hundred a week does wonders even here on the thirty-second floor. Now, shall we go?"

Barbara sighed. It was the one final grain of sand that overpowered her—his courtesy. Suddenly it all was too much for her. She felt her backbone melt and her resolve give way. After all, he did have a right. He had so many more rights than he was getting.

She nodded. "Yes, Roscoe, I think it's time. And I want Mr. Frost to come along as well." She smiled at Mark and motioned him toward the door. "I'm tired of playing this crazy game. It's too much for me. Jethro said it would be, but he insisted that I play along with it as long as I could."

She led the way out of her office, down the hall to a locked, shiny, stainless steel door. She used two keys, and when the door was opened, there was a guard who demanded a password. At last they were admitted into the hallway.

For all practical purposes they were in a hospital

corridor, starkly white, with three large-windowed rooms leading off it. She went in the first room and talked to a nurse, who smiled and left. The men edged inside.

A hospital bed had been turned so the person lying there could see the window, watch the lights at night and the lake by day.

There was no movement on the bed. Mark moved to the window side and was surprised at the thinness of the man's face. It was as if death had been cheated, had missed this man who had already passed over, but his body was still breathing, his heart beating, and his flesh withering away. The skin was so tight it must hurt to move his mouth, skin stretched over prominent cheekbones, and sunken blue-black recesses showed where clouded eyes lurked.

"Jethro, I've come back to see you tonight because we have excellent news. Roscoe wants to thank you for the present you arranged for his birthday, the sailing boat *Courageous.*"

Mark could see no movement from the corpselike form lying on the white sheets. Had the eyes moved? Mark thought not. Then he saw one bony hand slide to a button on the side of the bed. The hand traveled only three inches, but the effort seemed to tire the man. He touched the button twice, and a computer readout screen over his head flashed the word, "Yes."

Mark concentrated on the eyes. They were frozen in place, dead windows on the world. So he was blind, almost one-hundred-percent paralyzed, but he could hear. He communicated by the age-old method of one squeeze for "no," two for "yes"—only now with computer sophistication.

The girl went on talking, brushing strands of errant white hair from his forehead. Then she touched his good hand lightly. He had been flashing "Yes" and "no" to her questions, and Mark realized it was all like a computer: the operator and the machine, a question, and the computer often answering with a "yes" or a "no."

They stayed for five minutes. Roscoe had taken a first long look at his father, then faded out of the room and into the hall. Mark found him shivering and shaking in a chair the nurse had provided.

"Why didn't you tell me he was practically dead? Why?"

"He told me not to," Barbara said. "He's still alive, alert. You'd be surprised how quick and sharp his mind is. Only his body has failed him."

"How in hell can he run Bainbridge Technical?" Roscoe thundered. "There's no way he can do it in his condition."

"We run it through the computers. We programmed into them everything he knows. It took us over three years."

Roscoe stood now, shaking his head. "I had no idea he was so bad, no idea at all."

"Now you know, Roscoe. What are you going to do? Will you go to the board and demand your inheritance and vote his stock, then elect yourself president and chairman of the board?"

He watched her for several seconds, and his shoulders sagged. "No, I should. I might have been able to at one time. But Dad never pushed me, never worked me through the management chain. I don't know the company well enough to run it." He brightened. "But I do know boats, I'll have a seat on the board, and I'll spend the rest of my time sailing. The *Courageous*, my God, what a coup, what a boat! How much did he pay for it? No, it doesn't matter, not if she's mine!"

They left Roscoe at the elevator and went back to

her office. Barbara mixed herself a drink at the small wet bar and took a long pull from it before she asked Mark if he wanted something. He shook his head.

"I'd rather you tell me about it. How it all started. This living death wasn't your idea, was it?"

She settled down on the sofa, kicked off her shoes, and tried to relax. Then she began.

"I came to work for Bainbridge originally as a computer lead programmer. Soon I became the chief programmer for the corporate office. I set up the most complex and difficult series of programs and trained others in how they worked. Jethro Bainbridge was in the forefront of the computerization of work loads and business procedures. He had some of his plants computerized before most firms even knew what a computer was.

"He put me to work to computerize the whole conglomerate. I was hard at work hiring people and setting up systems when he had his first stroke. It hit him hard and left half of his body paralyzed for three months. Only a few of us knew about it. When he recovered, he said he realized he wouldn't live forever. But he had plans.

"He took me off the other work, and together we began to create the smartest, the most practical, the greatest business computer memory bank in the world. We put in everything that was Jethro Bainbridge. It included his business philosophy, his techniques for handling people—executives, vice presidents, secretaries—everything he had learned in a business lifetime. We got into day-to-day running of the office, put in problems that we had never heard of, and worked out solutions. By the time we were done, after more than three years, that memory bank held more of Jethro Bainbridge than we both ever imagined it could. We had captured his whole business personality, his business ethic, and his way of life.

"I don't think I would have stayed if I had guessed what he was really trying to do. He wanted the computer to replace him if he died suddenly or if he had more strokes. About a year ago the strokes began again, and six months later he was in the condition you just saw. He's helpless, fed intravenously, and his body will never move again."

"Then you and the computer have been running Bainbridge Technical for the past six months?"

"Yes. And sometimes I really don't believe it myself. When a management problem comes up, I ask the computer what to do. If it's covered and the computer printout seems a practical solution, I pass it along to the proper operating vice president as orders from Mr. Bainbridge. Gradually they couldn't get in to see Jethro. He had the hospital wing all set up a year before he needed it, the staff there on full pay. It was our glorified first-aid center and emergency room but wasn't used much until he took it over six months ago. Now no one else is ever there as a patient.

"He knew his time would come. He had projected his own infirmities and predicted almost to the month when he would have his bad strokes."

"But in the highly competitive field of electronics and miniaturized components . . ."

"I know, but it's worked up to now. The field is so fast moving that things are happening now we didn't even guess might come for another ten years when we programmed the computer just eight months ago. So we're becoming archaic."

"Extortion—did Jethro have an answer to that?" Mark asked.

"Of course." She went to the computer terminal and

punched in the question. A few seconds later the answer came on the screen.

"EXTORTIONISTS ARE LIKE BLACK-MAILERS—NEVER PAY THEM A DIME. KILL THEM IF YOU CAN. THAT'S THE ONLY REASONABLE WAY TO DEAL WITH A BLACK-MAILER OR AN EXTORTIONIST."

"And those are the exact words that Jethro Bainbridge used when we talked about it. In a way that man will never die."

"And now? What about you?"

"First we catch the extortionist, and then, if we have a building and a company left, I'll show you what I'm going to do."

Mark stood. "It's almost eleven, and I have a late date. I'll see you tomorrow."

She frowned and looked up at him quickly. "You're seeing a woman, now?"

He smiled shaking his head. "No, actually I'm going to practice the gentle art of breaking and entering. There's a certain computer store I want to break into."

Mark left, knowing she didn't believe him.

Chapter 14

YOU ALL WILL DIE!

The Penetrator glued himself to the brick wall in the alley behind the Bytes & Chips electronics store. A drunk staggered into the mouth of the ally fifty yards away, looked around in surprise in the darkness, turned, and stumbled twice before he negotiated the six feet back to the sidewalk. He waved a little, mumbling to himself, and moved on past the alley mouth.

Mark eased away from the wall and ran to the back door of the electronics store owned by Danny Danlow. He had his picks out and in twenty seconds opened the simple lock and stepped into the store. He heard no alarms, saw no special lights, and, as he paused, crouching beside the door, he heard nothing unusual in the small back room. It was jammed with stacks of boxes filled with expensive electronic components, computers, terminals, new screens, and print-out devices.

He wasn't interested in the hardware or the software programs. What he wanted were the company's records, sales, books, ledgers, anything down on paper. The office where he had talked with Danlow had a twin on the other side of the display room. The other office held the business end of the operation: a number of office machines, a typewriter, a small computer readout screen and terminal, and various stacks of account books.

Mark checked the books quickly. He knew now what name to look for. In accounts receivable under the L's he found the name of Hector Lattimer. One portable computer terminal. The first note showed it as sale, with $500 down and balance due. Then the sale entry was crossed out and the word "rental" printed beside the typing. There had been another payment of $1,500 and under this one was a notation: "10% fee per action." Ten percent of what? What action? At least, he had made a firm connection between Lattimer and Danlow.

He walked back into the showroom and felt a cough coming on. Mark wasn't used to the cold Chicago weather yet. The cough exploded harshly and loudly.

At once a floodlight snapped on, and a voice boomed into the room.

"Stop! Do not move. You are in an area controlled by sound-sensor devices. An automatic signal has been sent to our protection agency. You cannot escape."

Mark grinned. The advances of science. The recorded voice came from three speakers, and the whole thing had been activated by the sneaky sound sensors, the same kind they had used in 'Nam. He sprinted for the back door, slid out, let it relock, and saw headlights turning into both ends of the alley. Trapped: Mark at once went straight up the vertical side of the brick back wall like a fly. He had learned the vertical climb years ago, and had used it many times to get out of jams. The rough brick offered plenty of finger-

and toeholds as he worked upward steadily. It was only a one-story building, and he was over the lip of the building and onto the roof before the cars came to a stop near the store's back door. Their headlights flooded the back wall and door.

The alley had a solid line of one- and two-story buildings both ways to the street. Anyone in the alley would have been seen and trapped. It was a good defense and must usually work. He heard noises now from the front. Tires skidded on pavement. Car doors slammed.

You couldn't fault Danny Danlow on his security. It couldn't have been more than two minutes after the sensors picked up his cough until the men were in the alley behind the store. The two men met at the back door, unlocked it, and went inside with guns drawn.

There was no sound from the store, and five minutes later the men came out, talked a moment about the lousy hardware that still wasn't working right, and drove away.

Mark went over roofs until he was almost at the alley mouth. He had seen no one in the alley or anyone watching it. He went down the vertical wall easily, dusted off his hands, and walked to the street and down two blocks where he caught a cab.

The Danlow connection still bothered Mark. Was there more behind it than Danlow's simply furnishing computer terminals, expertise and components, to rip-off artists, computer style?

He had given the cabby the address where Hector Lattimer lived. It was a long shot, but this case was full of surprising long shots. Mark got out of the cab a block from Lattimer's apartment house and walked past the building on the other side of the street. There were two cars with blobs in them that probably were police stakeouts. The cops should be here if they acted on the information about Lattimer they had received. Mark came toward the alley from the far side, saw a plainclothesman halfway down the strip of cement, and kept on walking. The police had the apartment tied up neatly. If Lattimer tried to come back for the computer terminal, they would grab him. He hoped they got Lattimer *before* he planted his bombs, not afterwards.

Mark took another walk, hoping he would spot Lattimer's brother, Monty, but the addict didn't seem to be lurking around the area. Mark knew there was nothing else he could do now, so he walked a few blocks to a phone booth and called a cab.

Hector Lattimer was not at his old apartment nor in his new room a mile away. He was in a storefront opposite the Bytes & Chips electronics store. He had planned on going to his new hotel room as soon as he got off the bus from Elgin. Instead he took a taxi to Danny's store and positioned himself across the street out of sight. He had an eerie feeling about the place, that something was going to happen there tonight, so he waited. A half hour later he had seen the two cars roar up to the front of the store and three men go charging inside. It had to be the electronic watchdogs that Danlow had bragged about installing. Had someone been inside or had the audio "fence" malfunctioned again?

Hector had watched Danlow turn the system on one night, so he knew how to turn it off. Now if he could only get inside the front door quietly, he would be set.

The security team inside the Bytes & Chips store was gone. Things returned to normal on the street.

Just after 1:00 A.M., Hector went to the front of the store and checked the lock. It was an old-fashioned one. With a simple pick and tension bar he had made

132

at his hotel room, he opened the lock, smiled, and went inside.

From then on it was routine for an electronics engineer. He turned off the audio alarms, hooked up one of the portable computer terminals in the shielded back office, and settled down to work.

From his pocket notebook Hector found the information he needed: the direct dial telephone number to connect him with the building services computer in the basement of Bainbridge Tower. The number worked correctly the first time.

Even here there was a required code number for activity. That was so some random dialer with a terminal couldn't get the computer into action and cause trouble. Hector punched in the clearance number on the terminal typewriter and got back approval and a request for a process.

The instructions he had for the computer went quickly. He ordered a change in maintenance procedures for the elevators that went from floor one to thirty-two. Work would start at 1900 hours on 14 February. The six elevators would be shut down at 7:00 P.M. for servicing and repair.

He then authorized a delivery by the freight elevator at the same 1900 hours on the same date: four large crates. The ten-foot-long by four-foot square boxes were to be moved to the third subbasement upon arrival.

Hector laughed softly as the computer acknowledged each group of instructions and asked for a new process. He had one more.

"All service and maintenance personnel are to be excluded from subbasement floor three after 1930 hours, 14 February, for a period of four hours. Due to danger, the whole third subfloor must be cleared of all personnel."

". . . CLEARED OF ALL PERSONNEL." The printout recorded the computer's readback of the order. Then it chattered again.

"WHAT PROCESS?"

Hector turned off the terminal, replaced the phone hand set, and tore off the printed copies of his messages, which he put in his inside jacket pocket. He returned the portable terminal to stock and flipped on the alarm system. He moved silently through the back room out the back door, making sure it locked. The rest of his work he could take care of later this morning by phone. No! Why not call her right now?

He waited until he reached the lobby of his hotel before he made the call. The lobby was warm, and he took off his overcoat and one glove before he dialed. The phone rang seven times before she picked it up.

"Miss Simpson? I hope I'm not disturbing your sleep, but I had to talk to you."

"What? Yes, you did wake me. Who is this?"

"You owe me twenty million dollars, Miss Simpson. You have been a terribly bad girl about the whole thing."

Her voice took on a strong tone. "Then you're our extortionist, our bomber, our murderer. We know all about you. You once worked for Bainbridge Technical. You're an electronics engineer. We know about your accident and your withered right hand. Mr. Hector Lattimer, we have no intention whatsoever of giving you twenty million dollars. Is that clear?"

"How did you . . ." He stopped. The shock of hearing her speak his name nearly made him slam the phone down, but that would be admitting who he was. "This name, Lattimer, was it? I'm not him. But I do hate Bainbridge Technical. You now have until noon today to get that twenty million into my Swiss bank. If you don't, you will die along with half the

134

people in Bainbridge Tower. Oh, I'll plan on setting off my bomb when as many people as possible will be working, so I can trap thousands and kill as many as I can. And it will all be on your conscience, Miss Simpson!"

"You're bluffing, Mr. Lattimer. We know you. We've had psychological profiles run on you, talked to your doctors. And they say you're a paranoid schizophrenic and that basically you're harmless. Hector Lattimer simply couldn't do these things."

"But your doctors are wrong! I did. I did blow up those buildings, and I'll blast a dozen more, killing more people each time until you cave in and pay me."

"We can't. The board of directors will not allow it."

"*Then thousands will die!* You'll never know when I'm going to attack. It might be at 8:00 A.M. in just a few hours. It might not be for a month or a year from now. Think what it will cost you in extra guards, extra worry. And you'll never stop me. You tell old Jethro Bainbridge that! He told me I was hurt in the line of duty for the good of the company and I would never be fired. Then two years later he did fire me. Retired me."

"He probably never knew about it," Barbara said. She sensed a chink in his armor. "I'll talk to him about you tomorrow. I'm sure I can get you reinstated. You have an excellent work record. Why don't you come to my office and we'll talk about you coming back to work?"

"Oh, no. Not me. You won't trap me that easy. No, no! I'm going to bury you. I'll kill you all! I'll have my vengeance. Nobody can deny me that. Then I'll go and spend all the money I have. You'll die; all of you working in Bainbridge Tower will die when I blow it up! *You all will die!*"

Chapter 15

A THIRTY-TWO-STORY BOMB

On February 14, Mark and Barbara spent most of the day touring the likely trouble spots in Bainbridge Tower. They had the electrical switching room sealed so tightly that not even a volt could sneak in or out. The heating and plumbing control rooms were checked, given special guards, and the men were told of the threats and instructed not to be afraid to use their weapons.

By noon both Barbara and Mark were tired. But they kept going and guessing.

"It's a giant puzzle. We don't have the slightest idea where he will strike," Barbara said over a late lunch. She toyed with her crab salad.

"It logically would be at some vital point," Mark said. "He mentioned to you something about 'trapping' as many workers as possible. That would indicate an attack that would bottle up everyone above the attack point."

Her eyes glistened for a second, and she looked up at him quickly. "You were in the army?"

He nodded. "Vietnam."

"Thought so. You talk just like . . . like someone I used to know." She looked away, and Mark sensed she had suffered a great loss.

Mark tried to lighten the mood and to brush aside the hurt in her eyes as he hurried on. "No, we simply keep searching watching, and looking. If nothing happens today, then we work out long-term protection plans. But your company psychiatrist said it was probable that Lattimer will attack as soon as possible. The doc told me that this type of kook is unstable and impulsive, but above all he is impatient. I think his try will be today or perhaps tonight. His talk about trapping workers may have been a false lead. Remember, Hector Lattimer is a near genius by his I.Q. rating, and he's above all a practical engineer. He'll work out his plan to perfection and try to carry it out."

She sighed. "That's what bothers me the most. If he were stupid and bumbling, it would be much easier to catch him."

By 5:40 P.M., they both were dragging. Every possible and logical spot for a bomb had been checked and double checked. Guards had been posted, and vital utility points were double guarded. Mark urged Barbara to get a hotel room for the night, but she refused and went back to her thirty-second floor office.

Mark took one fast cruise past the Lattimer apartment building. The same cars seemed to be on stakeout, only this time one of the cops was having a takeout lunch. Mark directed the cab to the Bytes & Chips electronics store. He would go in and confront Danlow about the use of his terminal in an extortion-and-theft ring. It might be enough of a threat to him to blow the whistle on Lattimer. Mark got out of the cab across the street from the store and paid the hack.

137

He was about to walk toward the computer store when he saw a man who looked exactly like Hectotr Lattimer's picture go into the store. It had to be Lattimer. Mark couldn't follow him in. Danlow might see him, and in a second he would have Lattimer out of there.

So Mark waited in the shop across the street and went in for a cup of coffee where he had waited for Danlow that first day. Lattimer could always skip out the back door, but Mark was betting that he wouldn't. Lattimer had nothing to fear, no reason to be furtive at this point. It was 6:15 P.M. when Lattimer left the store. He had a package under his arm and at once caught a cab. Mark almost lost him, but at last got a cab, and the driver enjoyed the game of trying to catch the other taxi. When he did, he hung in behind Lattimer's hack, one car away, just like in the movie wild chase scenes.

Soon it became evident the cabs were heading for the part of town where Bainbridge Tower was situated.

A few minutes later the cab ahead pulled up at the side entrance to the Tower. Mark's hack stopped fifty feet behind. When Lattimer got out of the taxi, he looked entirely different. He had on a better hat and wore a fake moustache and beard and dark glasses. Mark paid the driver as he saw Lattimer vanish into the Tower. It must be tonight!

Mark tailed Lattimer. He went in an employee entrance on the lower level, flashed a badge, and got past the guard. Mark had to dig out his letter from Barbara and nearly lost Lattimer again as the guard checked the letter critically. Mark had to run down the corridor so he wouldn't lose Hector.

The route wound down to subfloor one, then to subfloor two, where Lattimer went into the men's room. Mark waited outside, grabbed a mop, and began swabbing the floor. It didn't matter; no one seemed to be using the hallway.

At last Mark put the mop back where he found it and retreated to the far end of the hall and waited. It had been half an hour since Lattimer went into the restroom.

It was nearly 7:30 P.M. when someone came out, and Mark did a quick double take. It was Lattimer but without his disguise. He seemed to walk with more purpose, heading for the stairs. Mark ran for the same stairs and got there just in time to see the third subfloor door closing.

Mark edged the heavy fire door open and saw Lattimer walking toward the elevators. The Penetrator wished he could simply jump the man, tie him up, and turn him over to police, but it would be too risky. Lattimer might already have planted his bombs; he might have set the timers and even now be checking their positions. If so, he would lead Mark right to the bombs.

From his hiding place Mark could see half of some large crates that had been placed near the bank of elevators. Each crate had writing on it, but Mark couldn't make out the small lettering.

Lattimer went to them, took some small tools from his overcoat pocket, and worked at the wire fasteners on the end of the crates. Were the bombs in the crates? How could they do much damage here? There was nothing on the third sublevel but storage, some open areas, and a whole floor full of building maintenance supplies and equipment.

Mark decided to wait. He had to know what type of device Lattimer was using; then he'd have a chance to handle it so it didn't get set off accidentally.

From one of the big crates Lattimer took a roll of six-inch flexible tubing. So the big crates were not the bombs. They must hold equipment to use to make the bombs. Mark was in time to stop him. Mark started to pull open the door when he heard a noise on the stairs behind him.

"Don't move. This is a cocked and loaded revolver, and it's aimed precisely at the middle of your back," a voice said. "I couldn't miss from this range if I tried. Put your hands against the wall and spread your legs. Don't move or you're dead. Some nut is trying to blow up this place, and it's probably you."

"Let me expl. . . ."

"Shut up! I don't want to hear a word from you. Move. Get against the wall, quickly!"

Mark scowled. He couldn't afford to waste much more time, but he had to wait until the guard was within striking distance.

"Officer, I'm here on business. I work with Barbara Simpson. I was all over this building with her today."

"Maybe yes, maybe no. Couldn't prove it by me, cowboy. I just came on the 6:00 P.M. shift, and tonight the brass got elbows up their noses worrying about this bomber guy."

Mark saw him then, a kid of twenty-five perhaps, fifty pounds overweight, sloppy, but he held the five-inch barreled .38 like he knew what to do with it.

"Hey, this is just like in 'Nam. You ever there?"

"All over that sewer, were you?"

"Hell, yes!" Just as the guard started to pat down Mark's legs with one hand, he leaned down, and Mark's right heel shot upward, catching the guard on the side of the head, slamming him backward. The revolver flew against the cement wall and fell without firing. Mark surged backward, grabbed the .38, and took the guard's handcuffs off his belt and snuggled one around the guard's wrist. The other cuff he fastened to the steel pipe railing along the stairs. The guard blinked and groaned.

"Lordy, what hit me?"

"Don't worry about it," Mark said. "Just keep quiet, and this will turn out fine."

Mark pulled the door open. Lattimer had been working quickly. Now all four of the big crates were connected to the elevator shafts with the large tubes. He was going to release something into the elevators. Why? Mark heard a hissing and looked at the nearest crate. Steam vented from a cap on top. Some wrappings had been removed, and now Mark could read the printing on the side of the big metal cylinder: "DANGER LIQUID HYDROGEN."

Hydrogen, a highly flammable gas. In liquid form it was tremendously compressed. When the liquid hydrogen in those four big cold bottles changed into gas and expanded, there would be enough to fill the elevator shafts a dozen times over, making a huge bomb! Liquid hydrogen had something like a fifty-thousand-to-one expansion ratio if Mark remembered correctly.

Mark had to stop this madman. He took one more look and saw that Lattimer had completed working with some wires on the first tank's valving.

Mark drew his .45 and jumped past the door and ran forward where Lattimer could see him.

"Drop the wires, Lattimer. Your little game is over. Move one inch, and I'll put six .45 slugs through your gut so you can die slow and painfully."

Lattimer jumped in surprise, looked up, and shook his head.

" 'Lazarus Laughed'—remember that? A play, I think it was. Lazarus died, and in the Bible he was raised from the dead. So later when he was threatened with death, it held absolutely no fear for him. He had been dead; he didn't fear death. I'm half dead now,

141

whoever you are. I don't fear death. There's no way you can stop me. I make one more connection, and then it's armed and ready. The detonators are on the valves, just big enough to knock off the valve on each of the cryogenic bottles, permitting the liquid hydrogen to jet through the tubes, expanding and turning into hydrogen gas and drifting up to the top of all thirty-two floors through the elevator shafts. Then when, by precise timing, the bulk of the hydrogen gas is in the elevators, another timer closes and sets off the detonator. You know what happens then? This whole damn Bainbridge Tower will explode like a dynamite bomb thirty-two stories tall! Can you imagine that?"

"But you won't see it because you'll be dead, Lattimer."

"Lazarus laughed at death. So do I."

The timing was wrong. He was seconds too late. That damned security guard. Mark had to stop any of that dangerous hydrogen from being released. Mark walked toward the first bottle.

"Hold it right there, or I'll connect these wires."

"You just touch the wires, and I'll blow your head off," Mark said, lifting his .45 to center on Lattimer's mouth.

Then something went wrong.

A valve broke. Fluid hissed out from the first huge cryogenic bottle and cascaded through the tubing. The pressure blew off the tube, and liquid hydrogen jetted directly into the opened elevator shafts in front of it. The liquid turned to a gas before it traveled far, most of it vanished into the chimneylike draw of the elevator shafts. The hissing turned to a roar.

Mark held his fire. Just one spark, and the whole place would blow sky high like a thirty-two-story cylinder of nitroglycerin!

Chapter 16

FIRE-STORM TRAUMA

Mark ran toward Lattimer, who fumbled with the wires. He tried to grab one wire with his injured right hand. But the dead hand wouldn't respond, and the wire slipped past the curved gloved fingers and fell to the floor, rolling back toward the bottles.

"It's working; it's working!" Lattimer screamed over the roar of the escaping gas.

"It isn't working," Mark shouted from six feet away. "All high-rise elevators must have vent fans in the shafts directly to the outside. It's the law. All of the hydrogen gas is being pumped directly to the outside at the fifth floor level and then again at floor ten. Nothing will get any higher."

"Lie, you lie. I ordered the computer to turn off those vent fans."

"It didn't work. The computer is safety oriented. That's its primary function, safety. Everything else is built on that base. This order was against its best safety programming. It took your instructions, but rejected them when it came time to order the work done. It's on our records in the computer log upstairs. That's how we knew you were coming here tonight."

"You couldn't have known. I told no one."

"Danny Danlow told me. He ratted on you, spilling his guts rather than have his parole rescinded. You don't have any friends left, Lattimer."

"Danny wouldn't do that."

Mark knew he had to keep the man talking. The roar of the escaping gas was down to a whoosh now. The vent fans above really were pulling the gas upward. Mark only hoped they were vented to the outside. He'd been bluffing Lattimer, but it must be true. More time, he needed more time for the gas to disperse, thin out.

"Danny did rat on you. And your kid brother, Monty, your dope fiend brother. He showed me where you lived, and we found the printout on your portable computer terminal. That's where you made your big mistake. Then we knew who you were and how you stole the money."

"You found it? Then those were cops outside my old apartment. I almost got out of the cab, but they changed my mind." He reached in his pocket and drew out a Colt .38 Super. "I have a gun, too, whoever you are. Just one shot into the elveator shaft should provide enough sparks. I see you're not going to give me the time to set up the other bottles correctly."

"A shot wouldn't do it now, Lattimer. Two or three minutes ago, maybe, but not now. The gas is too thin, like in your car. The spark won't fire the gas. You're too late."

Mark knew it wasn't too late, but he had to stall. "What about the girl, Iris McGrew? Why did you kill her? That was another mistake. I almost caught you that night."

144

"She was a nobody. I needed the numbers; she gave them to me, and I didn't need her anymore. Then she called me names and tried to phone the police. It was her fault that she died. It was all her fault. If she'd been quiet and not hysterical, she'd be alive today. A little smarter and more experienced but at least alive. It was her own fault."

Lattimer looked at Mark, then at the cryogenic bottle. The hissing of the gas was down to a gentle rushing sound now, and the hydrogen-saturated air hurt Mark's lungs. He didn't know why. Perhaps there was not enough oxygen left in the air.

"Don't try to follow me, whoever you are," Lattimer said. "I'm going into the space by the elevator, and I'm going to shoot into it. There's got to be enough gas left there for a good explosion, and that one will trigger another one and another one. It won't be the massive effort I planned, but it should work. And remember, Lazarus laughed." He staggered as he started to walk toward the elevator behind him.

Mark's eyes watered. His arms felt as if a hundred pounds were in each fist as he tried to raise the .45. It weighed more than he had ever imagined. He had to shoot Lattimer. Had to stop him. Mark fired, but the room didn't explode. He saw the round miss Lattimer and crash into a cement abutment. There were no sparks. Lattimer walked faster now. Mark started the other way. He moved toward the stairs and the fire door. Fire, explosion, that damn fire storm! He tried to run for the door. Get out the fire door! Get out the fire door! Get out the damn fire door!

His mind hammered the instructions at himself through a foggy body that wanted to cooperate but had forgotten how. His legs were anchors sinking him into the concrete. His whole body struggled and staggered and cried out in pain as he mentally stormed toward the door but realized that he was barely shuffling along, hardly lifting his feet off the floor.

He could see the jet plane come over, a new model with twin napalm bombs on its wings. It was a training demonstration of why and how to use napalm. Mark saw the surprised look on the lieutenant's face. The officer screamed to his men to hit the dirt, to take cover. The pilot had dropped the bomb short, far short.

Mark dove into the ditch, the deepest part he could find, and at once three more men slammed into the same hole on top of Mark, crushing him, almost smothering him.

Five seconds later Mark felt the searing, gut-wrenching, lung-burning explosion of the napalm and then the unbearable blast of heat, the screams, the never-ending agony of his lungs begging for air in the sudden vacuum created by the fireball that devoured every molecule of oxygen it could find as the black cloud rose into the late afternoon California sky.

Pain, unendurable pain, and then the blackness descending until there was nothing left.

Later—they told him it was no more than a half hour—he heard voices. There were screams for medics. A jeep roared up, and as Mark felt the pain again he knew he was not dead. Weights were moved off him, and he heard muted voices. He lifted his arm.

"Goddamn! Hey, here's one alive. Get that stretcher over here. Get the oxygen quick. Move your ass, soldier!"

Mark never saw the three scorched bodies that had been on top of him that afternoon, the three men who had died as they unknowingly saved his life.

"Get out the damn fire door," he mumbled again as

he shuffled forward. "Get out the fire door!" It was a million miles away. He stumbled, his body begging for oxygen. Another step, one more, now another one. Move, dammit! Move or die!

Another step, and he touched the wall, two steps down to the door. He fell against it. No! He had to pull it towards him. Gingerly he moved off the door, teetered, and almost fell. He pulled the door outward. Over his shoulder he saw Lattimer standing in front of the open elevator shaft shooting into it. Once, twice, three times.

Mark fell through the opening to the hard cement and saw the door closing. Suddenly there was a flash and the door slammed shut against steel bracing and bounced several times. A sudden gush of heat poured under the narrow crack below the door. Then it was gone, and Mark panted as he leaned against the wall.

At least he was still conscious. Had it been an explosion beyond the door? Yes, he could remember it. Big enough, but not tremendous. And he was still alive.

Something was different. The air. The sweet, clean air. Odorless, colorless, the damn hydrogen gas he had been breathing was slowly starving him of oxygen. Mark shook his head. He knew his brain was short on oxygen, plenty of blood but not enough oxygen in it. The air felt good, smelled good!

People would be coming. He let that idea sink into his mind for a moment. He didn't know how long he sat there. Then he thought about his weapon. He still had the .45 in his right hand. No license for Chicago. Get rid of it. He knew he should get back to the door, push it open. He got to his hands and knees and crawled. His head hit the metal door. It was hot but not burning.

Slowly he pushed the door open a crack. Dark. He

realized the lights were also out in the stairwell. He threw the .45 automatic inside, let the door come shut, and rolled away. Sleepy, so damn sleepy. It must be the oxygen starvation again.

The whole third floor level had been dark, but he had seen several small fires. One in front of the elevator. Then he remembered what else he had noticed. The smell. The infuriatingly sweet odor of burning flesh. He had prayed that day on the mountain that he would never smell human flesh burning again. For a moment he thought he would vomit.

He heard voices from above. That made him remember the guard he had handcuffed to the stairs railing. Mark tried to laugh, but he couldn't. The guard would have had a key to his own cuffs. Mark hadn't taken it away from him. So the guard had unlocked his cuffs and gone for help.

Voices. A door opened above, and a shaft of light came down.

"Hey, anyone down there?"

Mark tried to call out but couldn't. His voice wouldn't work. He did feel stronger now. By the time the first man in a gas mask reached him he had recovered enough to sit up against the wall. The man in the mask helped him stand, slung him over his shoulder fireman style, and carried him up the steps to sublevel two.

In the corridor were several dozen people, guards, police, and civilians.

"This one is alive," the guard said, pulling off his mask. "He was in the stairwell. I ain't been into level three yet. Sure stinks down there. Some damn sweet smokey smell."

A guard with captain's bars on his shoulders edged into Mark's vision. His face spelled excop. "Anyone else down there?"

Mark nodded, tried to talk, but couldn't. He didn't know why. The security captain scowled. "Just what the hell were you doing down there? That's a restricted area."

Mark tried to answer, then saw movement, and Barbara Simpson flew through the crowd.

"Let me through. Stand back!"

Some of the guards recognized her. The captain did. He came upright at once.

"We have a survivor from the explosion area. Like I told you, Miss Simpson, it ain't half bad. One elevator got burned some, and that bank will be out for two or three days. Six doors got blown off on the floors above but nothing too bad."

"Yes, good. Later, Captain. Get your men into level three and see if they can find anyone else. This man is working closely with me. He's an expert on these affairs. Now get your men in masks and with plenty of stream lights, and get down there!"

"Yes, ma'am!"

Barbara sat beside Mark on the hallway floor. She told the others to get on with their jobs. Then she smiled at Mark.

"Was it Lattimer?"

He nodded slowly.

"I had a report on that four-story building in Elgin. Lattimer used liquid hydrogen, let the gas fill the building, and then set it off. Was that what he tried to do here?"

Mark nodded again, now more certain his head would not fall off. He didn't know why he felt so washed out, so dopey, as if he were on a hyperventilating trip. Yes, he did, oxygen starvation.

"Security said four big crates with cold bottles in them arrived here at 8:00 P.M. and went to sublevel three. Did he use all four of them."

Mark held up one finger.

"He used one?"

Mark nodded.

Someone knelt down beside Mark and took his pulse and peered at both his eyes with a small light. Barbara had made room for the man as soon as he came. *Medic,* Mark thought.

The doctor held up his hand. "How many fingers do I have showing?" he asked.

Mark tried to say two but couldn't, so he held up two fingers himself.

"Mmmmmm, alert, vision all right, hearing fine, pulse good, but damn slow at forty-eight. He must have a hell of a good heart."

"The hydrogen gas he's been breathing—could that have done him harm?"

"Hydrogen gas? Colorless, odorless, highly flammable, diatonic gas. Can't do much, just kill him. If he got a heavy enough intake, he has oxygen starvation. The hydrogen molecules pile up in the lungs, literally clogging the spaces where oxygen molecules are supposed to pass into the capillaries and on into the bloodstream. Works the same way with carbon monoxide, a buildup thing. Pretty soon no oxygen can get into the blood and the body starts to shut down."

He dug into his bag and brought out a small canister and a face mask. The doctor fitted the mask over Mark's nose and mouth and turned on the canister.

"Pure oxygen, same kind the football players use after a long run at Denver or after the Olympics in Mexico City. Steady and slow. Just breathe normally and don't try to take too much at a time."

When Mark came off the oxygen at the end of two minutes, he felt better. But he didn't try to talk. The lights came back on in the hallway, and everyone relaxed.

"Do you need to stay here any longer?" Barbara asked Mark.

He shook his head. He didn't want to try to talk yet. He had no idea what kind of tricks his oxygen-starved brain had played on him. The recall, the re-living of the training accident was something he hadn't done for years. He hadn't even thought about it lately. Twenty-one of the twenty-six-man detail had died in that dry, burned-out gully, including the lieu-tenant. He frowned and looked at Barbara. Had she said something?

"Frost, I think you better come up to my apartment and let Dr. Jennings examine you more completely. Can you walk, or shall I get a wheelchair?"

He shook his head and stood by leaning against the wall. He found that once he started, he could walk at about half his usual speed. City firemen streamed into the corridor, masks fixed, and ran down the stairs.

The guard captain came back and said all lighting had been restored in the building. "We found some startling evidence in the area that the police have cor-doned off."

"Later, Captain. The first thing I want you to do is get these damn bottles of liquid hydrogen out of the building. Give them to one of our chemical firms. Call one and have them get those bottles right now. I want them gone from this building within an hour at the latest!"

"Ma'am, but I'm just a guard."

"Sorry, Captain." She went to a wall phone and di-aled, talked a moment, then came back to Mark and the doctor.

"Let's get this man upstairs, Doctor. I want you to take a closer look at him. He's a very special person."

Chapter 17

CRYPTANALYST, FRONT AND CENTER

Upstairs, Barbara put Mark in her bedroom and told the doctor to give him a good physical examination. "I'm responsible for him, and I don't want any problem to slip by unattended." The doctor vanished into the room, and she paced the floor, took two telephone calls, and told the switchboard to hold any more. Then she waited.

A half hour later Dr. Jennings came out of the room, smiling.

"He's tough as an old leather shoe, that one," Dr. Jennings said. "A weaker man would have been dead. His body will throw off the effects of the hydrogen in a day or two. I want him to take pure oxygen for five minutes every hour. Outside of that, just some rest and tender care is all he needs."

"Doctor, can he talk now?"

"Yes. It was all psychological. Several years ago he was in an army training accident. Most of his platoon was wiped out when a napalm bomb fell on them. The fire and heat were awesome. He couldn't speak for a month after that happened. His mind triggered the same response, but we worked it out. From what he said he relived the whole thing while he was trying to get away from the explosion he knew was coming."

"Thank you, Doctor Jennings. Any other special care he needs?"

"No. In a day or two he should be almost as good as new. Have him come in and see me if you wish. I'll have them send over six oxygen bottles so you don't run out. Be sure to use the oxygen. If he sleeps through the night, don't wake him. But give him oxygen every hour during the day."

She thanked him, and he went back to the clinic on thirty-two where he monitored Jethro Bainbridge. Barbara opened the bedroom door quietly and stood there looking at Mark. He lay on her bed under a sheet, his stare following her.

"Feeling better?"

"Yes."

"I'm your special, full-time nurse."

"Loose ends. We have a lot of loose ends. . . ."

She stopped him by shaking her head and walking up to the bed.

"No, absolutely not. You are not to worry about anything but getting well. Rest—that's what you need now. Just close those deep, dark eyes of yours, and go to sleep."

A smile brushed his face, and he nodded. "First, one thing I need."

"What's that?"

"Something I've wanted to do ever since I met you."

"What?"

"Come down here."

She knelt beside the bed, and he leaned out and kissed her lips gently; then he lay back and closed his eyes. She watched in fascination, and in not more than thirty seconds he was sleeping.

Barbara smiled, remembering the softness of his kiss, and tiptoed out of the room, shut off the light, and closed the door.

She made a number of calls, found that all the small fires were out in the elevator shaft and that cleanup was underway. The firemen were gone, and the cryogenic bottles had been removed from the Tower and were safely stored in one of their chemical firms.

About 11:00 P.M. she had a call from Lieutenant Werner of the Chicago Police Department.

"Miss Simpson, we've made a positive ID on the victim of the fire in your building tonight. He's Hector Lattimer, all right. Strange thing about that fire that killed him. The only part of his flesh that was seriously burned was his left hand. It was charred and twisted until it looked almost like his withered right hand he had injured years ago."

"And have you tied him in with the McGrew killing?"

"Not yet. If only we had the fingerprints from that right hand."

"We can provide them. Lattimer had top security clearance, so we have a complete set of prints from both hands, prior to his injury."

"I'll have a man pick them up from your personnel department first thing in the morning."

"He did admit to me over the telephone last night that he had blown up one of our chemical plants and that small plastics factory in Elgin."

"Not much we could use there, but if those prints match, even the partials, we should have enough for our ten-point identification."

Later she talked to security, and everything had

settled down. Repair crews were working, and three of the east bank elevators would be operating by the time people came in the morning. The other three lifts would take more time.

Every half hour she checked on Mark, but he was sleeping, his body gradually countering the hydrogen buildup in his lungs and throwing off the effects of the oxygen starvation.

Two days later Mark was up and prowling the suite. Barbara refused to let him even think about working or leaving until Dr. Jennings had given him a release.

They had talked about a hundred things in the two days, and she had moved his things from his hotel room into her apartment. She didn't even ask about the heavy, identical aluminum suitcases.

Now she spread out on a table all the data on her current project. "Frost, how do I get back the six million dollars that Lattimer stole?"

Mark looked at the printouts and shrugged. "Simple. Use the same code numbers he did, and instruct Bankwire II to withdraw the five and a half million we know he deposited in his Swiss bank in Lausanne."

"I tried that. The code number he used on the printouts is for deposit only. We need the authorization code for a withdrawal."

Mark dropped into a chair and looked out over Lake Michigan. "That presents a problem, since the only man who knows the other code number is now in the first stages of feeding a variety of small grubs and worms."

"So what do we do?"

"You're the computer expert. We come up with the code he used. Knowing as much about him as we do, it should cut down the odds. Can the code be numbers as well as letters?"

"Yes, either one, or a combination of them."

"Great." He looked over Lattimer's personal history and work record file. "Okay, here's the first try: his birthdate: 7-4-40. Then reverse it to 40-4-7, and then throw in 40-7-4 and 4-7-40 and 4-40-7 and 7-40-4. Those are the six possibilities with that three number group. Then we can go with his initials the same way with the six combinations there, H.A.L., L.A.H., and so on."

"I'm impressed. You could work in our encoding division." She grinned. "Now let's try those twelve combinations and see what we get."

They went to her apartment desk, which had a small computer terminal. She opened it and quickly punched up the required numbers to get Bankwire II and initiated a process to withdraw the five and a half million from Lattimer's numbered Swiss account. When time came for the code word, she tried the six they had worked out on his birthdate, but none worked. Then she fed in the six on his initials, but again all were rejected.

They worked all morning with various combinations of numbers, with his parents' initials, with combinations of letters of his street, his house number, his parents' birthdays, the day of the month and year when he was injured.

Mark stood looking out at the lake. "It must be something close to him, something he would remember easily, that he couldn't possibly forget. What we need is a real cryptanalyst," Mark said. "A word or number code man—the military used lots of them, and the state department. You have any clout either place?"

She shook her head.

"One more try. Remember the old kid game of making codes by using the number of a letter in the alphabet as the letter? A becomes 1, F is 6, and so forth. What would that make his initials?"

She worked it out: "8-1-12," she said. "The computer doesn't believe in hyphens, so it becomes good old 8112." She keyed in the Bankwire II requests and punched up the bank in Lausanne. The process was a withdrawal of five and a half million dollars from Lattimer's bank to be deposited to the Bainbridge account in Chicago First City Bank. Then there was the same four or five-second delay they had agonized through with each of the tries. Mark stared out the window. Then the printout began chattering.

"TRANSACTION   COMPLETED.   WITHDRAWAL MADE, CREDITED TO FIRST CITY BANK, CHICAGO, USA, 5.5 MILLION."

"It worked!" Barbara squealed. "We did it! We stole that money back from him!"

Mark laughed as he watched her. Barbara had lost all her sheen and sophistication. She was a little girl again with a brand-new dress and an all-day lollipop, excited, thrilled, happy.

"I don't believe that we did that. I didn't see any way in a million years that we could hit the right code. Do you know what the odds are of doing that? He could have used up to seven digits and numbers and with ten numbers and twenty-six letters the potential combinations must be way up in the millions!"

She hugged Mark in total joy; then her mood changed, and she lifted her lips to be kissed. He kissed her, slowly, with more feeling than the other time. She sighed.

"Now that is the nicest thing you've said to me all day."

She moved away, still smiling. "I think he's recovered. You said there were several loose ends to tie up. I'd say we have just knotted one of the biggest ones. Five and a half million dollars isn't a bad morning's work!"

"True, but there still is most of that other $500,000 out there somewhere. As I understand it, the police haven't even searched his room. They had no cause. They found the portable terminal and identified the printout you gave them as coming from that machine. His prints were on it, and the prints from the Iris McGrew apartment matched his. So they had him. So they never got a warrant for the new place."

"And you think the cash is still there?"

"Yes. His name and hotel and even the room number were shown in your copy of the police report. I think I'll run over there and see what I can find."

"You mean break in and take the money?"

"If I find it."

"That's stealing."

"I'm only a beginner. You just stole five and a half million!"

"But that was the company's money."

"So is this. I'll be back in an hour."

It was as Mark had guessed. The police had no interest in Lattimer's current address. Mark had to wait only for one maid to leave the hall before he worked the lock and got inside quickly. He found the money in an attache case hidden inside another suitcase in the closet.

Mark was in and out of the room in five minutes. No one saw him either time, and now he carried the attache case openly, using the elevator and catching a cab.

Barbara stared at the case of stacks of hundred dollar bills and shook her head in amazement.

"I really don't see how you did it. You recovered almost six million dollars today."

"But it was stolen." They both laughed.

"Frost, and I don't believe for a moment that is your right name, I really don't think you work for the IRS. In fact I know you don't, because I talked to the top man in personnel in Washington, and he assured me they have no people who do what you say you do, and they have no employee with your name or ID number. Oh, don't be worried; I really don't care who you work for, or with, or why. I would like to know just out of curiosity, but a girl can't push her luck too far, and so far I've been tremendously lucky. We still have a headquarters building, thanks to you, and we recovered almost all of our stolen six million, thanks to you. And I've had the pleasure of getting to know you a lot better."

"Routine, fair princess. I always try to rescue damsels in distress whenever I can."

"Now you're teasing me. Frost, when we recovered that $80,000 a year ago, we gave the detective a ten percent finder's fee. I'm sure the board of directors would go along with the same percentage here. You could use the money, couldn't you? Say $600,000 that the IRS doesn't know anything about?"

"Probably. Oh, I wouldn't spend it on myself. I don't need much money for myself."

She was smiling and nodding. "I didn't think you would. Can't you tell me who you work with? Some kind of a foundation or a Robin Hood group? You're not government, I know that, but I can't get you figured out any better."

"Don't try. I'd really rather you just accept the aid and comfort and forget about the who or why. There's one more loose end we need to think about."

"Jethro?"

"Right. You said you'd make things right about him."

She went to her small desk and took out two pieces of paper. The letter had been single-spaced and beautifully typed on Bainbridge stationery. In it she told the members of the board of directors exactly what had been going on during the past six months and asked their immediate help. She asked them to convene a shareholders' meeting of the board to elect new officers and a new president and chief operating officer. In the end she offered her resignation but asked to be allowed to stay on in her capacity as computer technology controller.

Mark finished the letter and handed it back. "Now that was what I was waiting for you to do. I think now we've just about wrapped it up."

EPILOGUE

Mark sat up in the queen-sized bed and looked out the window at the glittering sea of lights. Chicago. Indeed it was a "toddlin' town," and he had seen quite a bit of it in the last two days with Barbara Simpson as his tour guide. The story of the extortion plan and computer bank fraud had hit the papers in a one-day surge and faded. The story of the factory bombings and the explosion and fire in Bainbridge Tower had lingered for another two days, but now it was already half forgotten by the public.

Mark leaned down and kissed the bare breast of the girl beside him.

"Can't you sleep?" Barbara asked him.

"I'm memorizing the lights from up here. Usually I don't get this view of Chicago."

"Trying to think of any more loose ends?"

"No, they're covered, all except one, and I know you'll do something about that when you can, through the board."

"Roscoe Bainbridge?"

"Yes, the poor little rich playboy and heir to the throne. What will happen to him?"

"He'll take over his father's voting shares, which is still such a big chunk nobody can ignore him. He'll sit on the board, attend meetings, try to take part. He'll be a good company man for three, perhaps four months. Then he'll realize how far out of his depth he is. He'll give his favorite on the board his vote proxies for three or four months at a time and go sailing.

"Roscoe will try to get the *Courageous* into shape for the next America's Cup yacht race. Roscoe will either make it on his own now or go quietly down the drain. My pick is that he'll settle down to the life of a wealthy playboy, sometime Board member, but more often sailing and trying to amuse himself. He will be happy."

"At least you've thought about him."

"The doctor today said that Jethro may live another five years. He's really not that old at seventy-six, and the rest of his vital signs seem to be good. Only someone has to tell him that he will no longer be running Bainbridge Technical. The notices went out to all stockholders with the legal eleven-day notification time about the stockholders' meeting. After that Jethro will be out. I don't want to tell him."

"Let the new chief operating officer do it."

"I probably will." She smiled at Mark in the semi-darkness. "Do you know what a fiddle-foot is?"

"No."

"It's an old western term, and that's what you are, Frost. A fiddle-foot is a person who has itching feet, who always keeps moving on. No roots, no permanent ties, a drifter. You've been as restless as a long-tailed cat in a room full of rocking chairs, as my old grandfather used to say. I know you're getting ready to move on. I can accept that. I don't know where you came from; I really don't know who you are or why you helped me and Bainbrdige. But I'm eternally thankful that you did. And now I can't very well get all teary-eyed and demand to know where you're going, or suggest that you take me along, or tell you to stay here, or say I'll scream and cry and wail if you leave. Which, of course, I will."

He kissed her lips softly and pulled her into the crook of his arm.

"You are one fine lady, Barbara Simpson."

She lay there silently for a while. "But you are going, right? You're going to leave tomorrow?"

"Yes."

She was quiet for a moment; then she turned and clung to him.

"I'm not going to say a damn word, and I'm definitely not going to cry." He felt her hot tears on his shoulder.

But she was right. Tomorrow he had planned to go flying to the West Coast for a quick recap on his next trouble spot. Earlier today he'd called Professor Haskins for an update on a situation he had been following. There was the whiff of a flagrant crude oil conspiracy that could bankrupt the United States in a matter of months and make the oil embargo of 1973-74 look like a minor inconvenience. The deal included a surprising number of huge U.S. oil firms and a few foreign suppliers. The plot had such far-reaching implications that it had to be rooted out, exposed, and smashed beyond repair. He would need all the skill and knowledge that he could bring to the problem.

Mark changed his mind. "Barbara, I'm not leaving tomorrow. I'm taking another day of vacation. One more day for you to show me the rest of Chicago. Another day to watch you smile and laugh, to watch you be serious, stern, and gentle."

She sat up, smiling now, and brushing the tears away.

"You won't be sorry. It will be a beautiful day and night, one that neither of us will ever forget."

It was.

THE PENETRATOR'S COMBAT CATALOG

If you've ever wondered about the Penetrator's weapons, his home base, his transportation, the Combat Catalog is designed to bring these vital elements in the Penetrator's career to you. This way you can keep up to date on his activities, and you can get the background on some of the weapons he has used in the past and probably will use in the future.

Some of the Penetrator's weapons are in action in one mission after another; yet he is always on the lookout for that special use gun that could give him the edge in firepower, accuracy, range, or surprise.

Each entry here includes the essentials about the weapon or item under discussion. If you wish to purchase any of these items from a reputable source in your area or from the factory, it is advised you first check local, state, and federal laws.

Good reading and best wishes.

Lionel Derrick

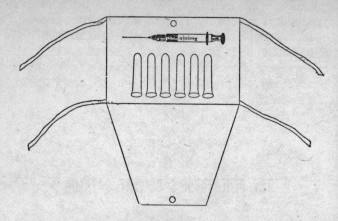

HYPODERMIC KIT

From time to time the Penetrator uses
a small hypodermic kit that can come
attached to his boot or lower leg. It is
a compact five-vial hypodermic needle
ready to use.

The color code of the injectables
have been matched with the loads on the
AVA dartgun darts.

    Blue vial.........tranquilizer
    Red vial..........death
    Yellow vial.......inert for
                         psychological uses
    Green vial........Sodium Pentothol
                  (truth serum)
    Brown vial........novacaine
                  (pain deadening)

  (Coding revised March 8, 1978, to
match AVA loading codes.)

The kit comes equipped with two, two-ounce hypodermic syringes, which are plastic and disposable. Additional ampules of each of the loads are kept in special padded packages in the assault weapons suitcases.

RIOT HANDCUFFS

Efficient, low-cost, disposable, and the simplest of the Penetrator's tools of his trade are these thin plastic strips that are used for emergency handcuffs. They are the same type as used by police when large groups of persons are arrested. The cuffs are simple strips of half-inch-wide plastic with a slit in one end. They come in many different configurations.

The long end of the plastic strip has reverse-cut notches in it. The notches slip forward through the slot as the cuffs are tightened around a person's wrists. The notches prevent the plastic strip from sliding backwards.

Such riot cuffs are used by the Penetrator as temporary restraining devices and usually with the victim's hands behind his back to prevent escape.

Riot cuffs come off a prisoner easily, and there is little discomfort associated with the plastic. The cost factor here is remarkably low. Generally not available to nonpolice groups or individuals.

M-79 GRENADE LAUNCHER

Mark's favorite heavy artillery piece is the old reliable M-79 grenade launcher borrowed from the military storehouse. Compact and light weight, it can throw out a variety of grenade type missiles from white phosphorous to high explosives over an effective range of up to 360 yards.

Regular hand grenades are not used in this weapon. Rather a special 40 mm "cartridge" is used which includes its own propellant similar to a shotgun shell. It's a shotgun type weapon that breaks apart for loading and is a single shot. The M-79 breaks down easily for storage and transport in Mark's famous aluminum suitcases. For harassment and destruction, Mark often fires white phosphorous and high explosive rounds alternately when laying down a field of fire against an entrenched or housed enemy. Not available to the public.

Specifications

Caliber: 40 mm
System of operation: single shot,
break-open type
Weight loaded: 6.45 pounds
Length: 28.78 inches
Length of barrel: 14 inches
Muzzle velocity: 250 feet per second
Sights: front, protected blade; rear,
leaf, adjustable for windage
Range: 360 yards maximum angle
Loading: Move barrel-locking latch
fully to the right and break open
breech. Moving latch to right automatic-
ally puts the weapon on "safe." Insert
cartridge in chamber until the extractor
contacts the rim of the cartridge case.
Close the breech. Push safety to forward
position exposing the letter "F." The
M-79 Grenade Launcher is now ready to
fire.

Assault Rifle configuration

Light Machine Gun

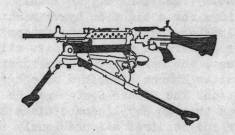

Medium Machine Gun configuration

STONER 63 WEAPON SYSTEM

Mark's Stoner 63 System is another
development of Eugene Stoner and is
being handled in the U.S. by the

Cadillac Gage Company of Detroit, Michigan. There are fifteen component assemblies, plus a machinegun tripod, in the Stoner System. Used in various combinations, this allows use of the weapon system as a rifle, a carbine, a light machinegun magazine or belt-fed or a tripod-mounted machinegun using either feed system. The system is so arranged that it fires from a closed bolt when used in the rifle and carbine configuration from an open bolt when used in the light and medium machinegun modes.

To achieve this difference, the hammer and timer used in the rifle-carbine configurations are removed and the vertical position of the bolt carrier and piston reversed. The unit is chambered in 5.56mm (.223), hardly an ideal cartridge for a light or heavy machinegun. Another drawback to the system is its preponderance of parts. Like all machines, the more parts to malfunction, the better chance of such a stoppage of operation. The Stoner System may be ordered through any licensed Class 3 dealer and requires all previously mentioned fees, licenses, and residence eligibility. No price available at time of printing.

Specifications

Caliber: 5.56mm (.223)
System of operation: Gas

Overall length: R. 40.25 inches
                Car: 35.87 inches
                LMG: 40.25 inches
                MMG: 31 inches
Sights: front, post with protective
ears; rear, aperture/lmg leaf with
aperture/fixed MMG, none
Barrel length: R. 21.67 inches; car.
15.7 inches; all others, 21.67 inches
Weight: R. 8.20 lbs; car. 8.1 lbs; Mag.
LMG 10.7 lbs; belt LMG 11.68 lbs; flex
MMG 10.13 lbs; fixed MMG 10.57 lbs
Muzzle velocity: (all) 3250 fps
Cyclic rate: R. 750-900/car. 740-800/
mag. LMG Approx 750/
Belt fed LMG 700-1000; flex. MMG 650-
850; fixed MMG 650-850 rpm

Performance

Except for the subcaliber chambering,
the Stoner System performs better than
most European or Soviet Block manufactured combination systems, with the
exception of the Heckler and Koch 7.62
NATO System. The quality of German
engineering and machining surpass Stoner
at nearly every point. The speed at
which the system can be altered from one
configuration to another is not considered a handicap in military situa-
tions, but for hit and run raids can
prove an obstacle.

Mark used his Stoner System in No. 10,

<u>Hellbomb</u> <u>Flight</u>, and has since retired
it to use as a belt-fed light machinegun
in the Stronghold's defenses. He has
since moved on to better and more adapt-
able weapons for rugged front line use.

WEATHERBY .460 MAGNUM DELUXE RIFLE

This long gun is used by Mark occasion-
ally for those jobs where a close-up
attack is not possible. The Weatherby
Magnum comes in either left- or right-
handed models. It will hold four rounds,
three in the integral magazine built
into the weapon, and a fourth round
pushed into the chamber. This weapon was
used by the Penetrator in book #16,
Deepsea Shootout.

Specifications:

Caliber: .460 magnum
Barrel: 26 inches
Weight: 10 pounds, 8 ounces without
sights
Action: Mark V
Nine locking lugs on enclosed bolt head
Special Pendleton muzzle brake
Bolt hand honed and damascened
Checkered bolt knob, engraved floorplate
Walnut stock, hand bedding, hand check-
ering
Swivels standard

THE YAQUA BLOWGUN

Blowguns are as old as man himself or
nearly so. Mark's 5-1/2-foot Hunter model
is manufactured by Green Hand Company
in Burns, Kansas. The principle of the
blowgun is simple; i.e., a projectile is
propelled down a hollow tube by a column
of air. Lung power most commonly pro-
vides the source of air; in modern
sporting blowguns, piano wire and
plastic "Hong Kong" beads of .38 caliber
provide the projectiles. Technique in
firing and gaining accuracy with a blowgun will be covered in performance
ratings.

NOTE: Possession of a blowgun is a
criminal offense in some states—California, for example—and anyone obtaining
one should check local and state regula-
tions before making purchase. On the
other hand, Oklahoma allows deer hunting
with a blowgun and poisoned darts,
determining them to be quicker, more
humane, than hunting bows.

Many sporting goods and discount
stores market sporting and survival
blowguns, or direct orders may be made
to the factory: Ole Green Giant, Box
62 PB, Burns, Kansas 66840. Suggested
retail price of the 5-1/2-foot Hunter
model is $14.95.

Specifications

Length: 5 foot, 6 inches
Bore: .41 caliber
Weight: 12-15 oz
Composition: aluminum tubing
Projectile: .38 caliber plastic bead
with piano wire shaft

Performance

An accomplished blowgun artist can
achieve 1-1/2-inch group accuracy at
ranges up to two hundred feet. With
practice of half an hour a day for three
weeks followed by ten minutes every
other day after that, an average person
can achieve remarkable results at ranges
from 75 to 150 feet. Blowgunning requires good hand-to-eye coordination and
the "trained" lips of a trumpet or trom-
bone player, pursing the lips and
"kicking" the air with tongue.

The air must be expelled sharply and
in large enough quantity to propel the
projectile through the bore and to the
target. A muzzle velocity slightly under
half of that of a .45 ACP round can thus
be obtained; some 400 fps and penetra-
tion of an inch or more can be achieved
in flesh, with half an inch common in
plywood or hardwood target backs.

Poison for dart tips can be obtained
from the manufacturer and employed where
legal for hunting. In the event of use

of poison, the game goes into convul-
sions in six seconds or under, expe-
riencing a reaction not unlike that
from nerve gas. The poison kills in
forty to eighty seconds, with no apparent
pain or trauma associated with arrowhead
or bullet wounds.

An insider's view of the *Death Merchant*— A master of disguise, deception, and destruction . . . and his job is death.

DEATH MERCHANT
by Joseph Rosenberger

One of Pinnacle's best-selling action series is the Death Merchant, *which tells the story of an unusual man who is a master of disguise and an expert in exotic and unusual firearms: Richard Camellion. Dedicated to eliminating injustice from the world, whether on a personal, national, or international level, possessed of a coldly logical mind, totally fearless, he has become over the years an unofficial, unrecognized, but absolutely essential arm of the CIA. He takes on the dirty jobs, the impossible missions, the operations that cannot be handled by the legal or extralegal forces of this or other sympathetic countries. He is a man without a face, without a single identifying characteristic. He is known as the master of the three Ds—Death, Destruction, and Disguise. He is, in fact and in theory, the Death Merchant.*

The conception of the "Death Merchant" did not involve any instant parthenogenesis, but a parentage whose partnership is more ancient than recorded history. The father of Richard Camellion was *Logic*. The mother, *Realism*.

Logic involved the realization that people who read fiction want to be entertained and that real-life truth is often stranger and more fantastic than the most imaginative kind of fiction. Realism embraced the truth

179

that any human being, having both emotional and physical weaknesses, is prone to mistakes and can accomplish only so much in any given situation.

We are born into a world in which we find ourselves surrounded by physical objects. There seems to be still another—a subjective—world within us, capable of receiving and retaining impressions from the outside world. Each one is a world of its own, with a relation to space different from that of the other. Collectively, these impressions and how they are perceived on the *individual* level make each human being a distinct person, an entity with his own views and opinions, his own likes and dislikes, his own personal strengths and weaknesses.

As applied to the real world, this means that the average human is actually a complex personality, a bundle of traits that very often are in conflict with each other, traits that are both good and bad. In fiction this means that the writer must show his chief character to be "human," i.e., to give the hero a multiplicity of traits, some good, some bad.

At the same time, Logic demands that in action-adventure the hero cannot be a literal superman and achieve the impossible. Our hero cannot jump into a crowd of fifty villains and flatten them with his bare hands—even if he is the best karate expert in the world! Sheer weight of numbers would bring him to his knees.

Accordingly, the marriage between Logic and Realism had to be, out of necessity, a practical union, one that would have to live in two worlds: the world of actuality and the world of fiction. This partnership would have to take the best from these two worlds to conceive a lead character who, while incredible in his deeds, could have a counterpart in the very real world of the living.

Conception was achieved. The Death Merchant was

born in February of 1971, in the first book of the series, *Death Merchant*.

This genesis was not without the elements that would shape the future accomplishments of Richard J. Camellion. Just as a real human being is the product of his gene-ancestry and, to a certain extent, of his environment during his formative years, so the fictional Richard Camellion also has a history, although one will have to read the entire series to glean his background and training.

There are other continuities and constants within the general structure of the series. For example, it might seem that the Death Merchant tackles the absurd and the inconceivable. He doesn't. He succeeds in his missions because of his training and experience, with emphasis on the former—training in the arts and sciences, particularly in the various disciplines that deal not only with the physical violence and self-defense, but with the various tricks of how to stay alive—self-preservation!

There are many other cornerstones that form the foundation of the general story line:

●Richard Camellion abhors boredom, loves danger and adventure, and feels that he may as well derive a good income from these qualities. The fact that he often has to take a human life does not make him brutal and cruel.

●Richard Camellion works for money; he's a modern mercenary. Nevertheless, he is a man with moral convictions and deeply rooted loyalties. He will not take on any job if its success might harm the United States.

●The Death Merchant usually works for the CIA or some other U.S. government agency. The reason is very simple. Richard Camellion handles only the most dangerous projects and/or the biggest threats. In today's world the biggest battles involve the silent but very real war being waged beween the various intelligence communities of the world. This war is basically between freedom and tyranny, between Democracy and Communism.

(The Death Merchant has worked for non-government agencies, but he has seldom worked for individuals because few can pay his opening fee: $100,000. Usually, those individuals who could and would pay his fee, such as members of organized crime, couldn't buy his special talents for ten times that, cash in advance.)

•The Death Merchant is a pragmatic realist. He is not a hypocrite and readily admits that he works mainly for money. In his words, "While money doesn't bring happiness, if you have a lot of the green stuff you can be unhappy in maximum comfort." Yet he has been known to give his entire fee—one hundred grand—to charity!

•Richard Camellion *did not* originate the title "Death Merchant." He hates the title, considering it both silly and incongruous. But he can't deny it. He *does* deal in death. The nickname came about because of his deadly proficiency with firearms and other devices of the quick-kill. (All men die, and Camellion knows that it is only a question of *when*. He has never feared death, "Which is maybe one reason why I have lived as long as I have.")

•The weapons and equipment used in the series do exist. (Not only does the author strive for realism and authenticity, but technical advice is constantly being furnished by Lee E. Jurras, the noted ballistician and author.)

Another support of the general plot is that Camellion is a master of disguise and makeup, and a superb actor as well.

It can be said that Richard Camellion, the Death

Merchant, is the heart of the series; but *action*—fast-paced, violent, often bloody—is the life's blood that keeps the heart pumping. This is not merely a conceptual device of the author; it is based on realistic considerations. The real world *is* violent. Evil *does* exist. The world of adventure and of espionage is especially violent.

The Death Merchant of 1971 is not necessarily the same Death Merchant of 1978. In organizing the series, we did use various concepts in constructing the background and the character of Richard Camellion.

Have any of these concepts changed?

The only way to answer the question is to say that while these concepts are still there and have not changed as such, many of them have not matured and are still in the limbo of "adolescence." For example:

We have not elaborated on several phases of his early background, or given any reasons why Camellion decided to follow a life of danger. He loves danger? An oversimplification. Who first called him the Death Merchant? What kind of training did he have? At times he will murmur, *"Dominus Lucis vobiscum."* What do the words "The Lord of Life be with you" mean to Camellion?

All the answers, and more, will be found in future books in the series.

Camellion's role is obvious. He's the "good guy" fighting on the side of justice. He's a man of action who is very sure of himself in anything he undertakes; a ruthless, cold-blooded cynic who doesn't care if he lives or dies; an expert killing machine whose mind runs in only one groove: getting the job done. One thing is certain: he is not a Knight on a White Horse! He has all the flaws and faults that any human being can have.

Camellion is a firm believer in law, order, and justice, but he doesn't think twice about bending any law and, if necessary, breaking it. He's an individualist, honest in his beliefs, a nonconformist.

He also seems to be a health nut. He doesn't smoke, indulges very lightly in alcohol, is forever munching on "natural" snacks (raisins, nuts, etc.), and uses Yoga methods of breathing and exercise.

Richard Camellion is not the average champion/hero. He never makes a move unless the odds are on his side. He may *seem* reckless, but he isn't.

Richard Camellion wouldn't turn down a relationship with a woman, but he doesn't go out of his way to find one. The great love of his life is weapons, particularly his precious Auto Mags.

As a whole, readers' reactions are very favorable to the series. It is they who keep Richard Camellion alive and healthy.

The real father and mother of Richard Camellion is Joseph Rosenberger. A professional writer since the age of 21, when he sold an article, he worked at various jobs before turning to fulltime writing in 1961. Rosenberger is the author of almost 2,000 published short stories and articles and 150 books, both fiction and nonfiction, writing in his own name and several pseudonyms. He originated the first kung fu fiction books, under the name of "Lee Chang." Among other things, he has been a circus pitchman, an instructor in "Korean karate," a private detective, and a free-lance journalist.

Unlike the Death Merchant, the author is not interested in firearms, and does not like to travel. He is the father of a 23-year-old daughter, lives and writes in Buffalo Grove, Illinois, and is currently hard at work on the latest adventure of Richard Camellion, the Death Merchant.